"Part of our tr[...] talk tonight,['...] sensually.

"You never said that before," Sadie protested lightly.

"Didn't I?" The corners of his eyes crinkled with amusement.

He really was heart-stoppingly sexy, Sadie acknowledged giddily.

"Ah well, I'm saying it now!"

"But if we don't talk about business, then what..." Sadie stopped and blushed as she saw the way that Leon was looking at her.

"Oh, I think we'll find that we have plenty of things to say to one another," Leon told her softly.

Sadie didn't make any reply. She was far too conscious that she was dangerously close to wanting much more from him than a simple business relationship!

GREEK TYCOONS

**They're the men who have everything—
except a bride...**

Wealth, power, charm—
what else could a handsome tycoon need?
In THE GREEK TYCOONS miniseries you
have already met some gorgeous Greek
multimillionaires who are in need of wives.

Now it's the turn of internationally popular
Presents author Penny Jordan,
with *The Mistress Purchase*.

This tycoon has met his match, and he's decided
he *has* to have her...*whatever* that takes!

Coming next month:

The Stephanides Pregnancy #2392
by
Lynne Graham

Penny Jordan

THE MISTRESS PURCHASE

GREEK
TYCOONS

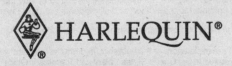

HARLEQUIN®

TORONTO • NEW YORK • LONDON
AMSTERDAM • PARIS • SYDNEY • HAMBURG
STOCKHOLM • ATHENS • TOKYO • MILAN • MADRID
PRAGUE • WARSAW • BUDAPEST • AUCKLAND

ISBN 0-373-12386-8

THE MISTRESS PURCHASE

First North American Publication 2004.

PROLOGUE

'EXCUSE me!' Sadie Roberts grimaced as her plea was ignored and she had to try to wriggle her way past the small group of men, all hanging fawningly on the every word of the man who was addressing them. And what a man, Sadie acknowledged with a small, irritated female surge of hostile and unwanted but still undeniably fierce awareness of him. If maleness was an essence, then this man possessed a potency that made Sadie's sensitive female receptors twitch warily.

He stood a good four inches above the older man who stood faithfully by his side, and whilst his voice was cool and low pitched it had a timbre that made Sadie shiver sensually, as though a soft, scented velvet glove had been slowly stroked over her bare skin.

Trapped where she was by the sudden surge of people trying to move down the narrow tented corridor that led from one part of the trade fair to another, Sadie wobbled perilously on her unfamiliar high heels—the shoes, like the heavy make-up, were her cousin Raoul's idea—and found herself being inexorably pushed closer to the arrogant stranger. So close, in fact, that she could have put out her hand and touched him. Not that she had any intention or desire to do such a thing. Had she? Wasn't she secretly thinking…wanting…? Frantically Sadie made a grab for her reckless thoughts.

He, the man she was tensing her body into denying its reaction to, had lifted his hand to look at his watch, its fingers lean, tanned, the nails neatly cut and clean, but still very masculine. It was a hand that belonged to a man who was fully capable of dealing competently with any number of manual tasks, whilst the suit he was wearing clearly identified that he was equally capable of writing a cheque to pay someone else to do them!

Oh, yes, he would be very good at writing cheques, Sadie decided. He had that kind of arrogance. A wealthy man's arrogance. It was there in the cool look of hauteur he was slanting over her; a slow, thorough visual inspection that was a disturbing combination of sensuality and slicing assessment.

Another rough push as someone else fought their way through the tightly packed crowd almost sent Sadie straight into him, so that their bodies might have meshed in a shared physical exchange that would sting her blood and stop her breath.

What was the matter with her? Why should she feel so alarmed, so unnerved, so…affected by the knowledge that beneath the cool silk mohair of the immaculate suit he was wearing surely lay a body that was all raw masculinity, solid hard muscle and sinew, all…?

Immediately Sadie froze, pushing away her unwanted and disruptive thoughts.

Irritated with herself and her uncontrollable reaction to him, she seized the opportunity provided by the thinning of the crowd and made herself walk away.

Hot-faced, she hurried back down the corridor in search of her cousin Raoul.

'Come here, Sadie, and let the guys get a whiff of our scent.'

Stony-faced, Sadie turned to face her cousin and co-director.

She was still furious with Raoul for the trick he had

pulled on her this morning, in persuading her to wear the perfume house's current scent. This was a scent created in Raoul's father's time—when he had briefly managed the small family-owned business. And even she was more annoyed with herself, for being gullible enough to fall for it. She should have listened to her own instincts and refused to go along with Raoul's plans the moment she had smelled the appalling concoction which was now offending her own olfactory senses! Instead, she had given in to a bout of sentiment and told herself that she wanted to do everything she possibly could to mend the breach in their family!

She had assumed that she was simply going to accompany Raoul to the trade fair. But Raoul had other ideas! The clothes, the make-up and the 'big' hairstyle he had bullied her into were bad enough, and just not 'her' at all, but she had bitten on her lip and given in—in the interests of cousinly harmony. But, oh, how she wished now she had not done so!

For the last few interminable hours she had been subject to a barrage of leering looks, suggestive remarks and totally unwanted physical intimacies from the would-be male buyers Raoul had persisted in inviting to sample the perfume she was wearing on her skin!

She loathed the scent. It was everything that Sadie detested most about modern synthetic-based perfumes, completely lacking in character and subtlety, with no staying power, and thin and cold where a perfume should be rich and warm, lingering on the senses like good chocolate or a lover's caress. And, even worse, this perfume had a brashness about it, a sexuality—there was really no other word—that Sadie personally found so loathsome that she now actually had a nauseating headache from wearing it!

'That's it. I've had enough. I'm going back to the hotel right now!' Sadie told her cousin grimly, as she evaded the unwelcome attentions of the red-faced overweight buyer who had been trying to nuzzle the side of her throat.

'What's wrong?' Raoul demanded, grinning slyly at her.

'What's wrong?' Sadie took a deep breath.

Eighteen months ago, on the death of her much loved maternal grandmother, Sadie had inherited a thirty per cent shareholding in the small prestigious French perfume house of Francine, which had been in her grandmother's family for several generations, along with the secret recipe for what had been the house's most famous scent.

Her awareness of the rift that had existed between her grandmother and her brother, Sadie's great-uncle and Raoul's grandfather, which had caused her grandmother to distance herself from the business and take no part in it, had initially coloured Sadie's reaction to her inheritance. But Raoul, who owned the remaining shares in the business, had invited her to heal the rift which had developed between the two branches of the family during her grandmother's time and not only take her place on the board but also put her skills as a perfumier to good use and work in the business.

But then she'd had no idea just how far from her own idealistic imaginings and dreams Raoul's plans for the business were!

Raoul, with his shrewd business acumen and lack of sentimentality, seemed determined to use every means he could to promote the perfume house, no matter how unsavoury or out of keeping with the house's history and traditions!

'What's wrong?' Sadie repeated furiously, her wide-set topaz eyes appearing pure gold with emotion. 'Do you really need to ask me that, Raoul? Can't you see how this…this publicity gimmick of yours is cheapening not just me but our perfumes as well? Do you really think that what I have just had to endure will encourage women to buy our scent? That by being pawed over by…by—'

'By the world's most influential megastores' perfume buyers?' Raoul cut in, the humour gone from his voice and his face set.

'I don't care what you say, Raoul,' Sadie told him. 'I'm going back to the hotel!'

Without giving him the opportunity to reopen the argument, she spun round on her heel and headed for the exit.

Initially she had been excited at the prospect of this trade fair, especially when Raoul had informed her that it was to be held in Cannes, which was so close to Grasse, where their great-great-grandfather had first begun his perfume business. But now she couldn't wait to get away and return home to her cottage in Pembrokeshire, over-looking the sea—and to her own burgeoning business, involving perfumes she made to order for a small group of discerning clients who came to her by word of mouth.

No, the world of big business most definitely wasn't for her—and as for the way that Raoul had set her up! Angrily Sadie hurried along the poorly lit tented walkway, too engrossed in her own thoughts to pay any attention to the small group of besuited businessmen hovering by the exit until one of them stepped in front of her, giving her a look of insolent sexual inspection before addressing his colleagues.

'Come over here and check out Raoul's latest offering, guys,' he invited.

Sadie froze, anger, contempt and disgust all burning into one hot golden fireball in her eyes as she flashed a look of fierce hostility at him. The height she had inherited from her father's family enabled her to meet the man's piggy-eyed leer, but a small quiver of female vulnerability still shuddered protestingly through her body.

The other men were surrounding her like a pack of jackals—not capable of hunting down their own prey, she decided, but all too eager to drag down and feed off someone else's. They were like vultures...

One of the men made a sexually abusive comment about her in French, causing Sadie to lock gazes with him in silent contempt. Thanks to her maternal grandmother, her own French was fluent and comprehensive, but there was no way she was going to lower herself to making any kind of response to what she had just overheard.

Instead she stepped sideways and, keeping her head held high, walked past the group of men, mentally promising herself that she would make sure Raoul knew exactly what she thought of him and his promotional ideas when he later returned to their hotel!

She was almost past the men when one of them suddenly reached out and grabbed hold of her arm.

Sadie was wearing a sleeveless black dress, and the sensation of the man's unwanted touch on her bare skin made her shudder and immediately pull herself free. Not only angry now, but also beginning to feel queasily apprehensive, Sadie kept on walking, her gaze resolutely fixed on the exit.

Which was no doubt why she didn't see the other man who suddenly loomed up at the side of her, having either bypassed or emerged from the leering crowd she had just escaped from.

She might not be able to see him, but she was immediately conscious of him, Sadie acknowledged as the felt the restrictive shadow his presence cast over her. And instinctively she knew! A sharp frisson of awareness shuddered through her, causing her to turn slightly towards him, even though she didn't want to. Her recognition of him was immediate—and shocking. His height and the breadth of his shoulders made her catch her breath, and she could sense too the alien and intensely male quality about him that had stopped her in her tracks earlier that day. Now it caused her to sway a little on her high heels as her body registered things about him that broke through her normal reserve.

She turned back sharply, determined to continue her journey. To her shock he lightly tapped her on the shoulder. Immediately Sadie swung round on her heels to confront him, her tawny gaze suddenly hazing as she realised just how far she had to look up before she could look into his eyes.

Just how tall was he? Six-two…six-three…four? He looked as though he might be Greek, Sadie recognised; he had olive skin colouring and the right kind of arrogantly and openly aristocratic good looks—the sculpted cheekbones; the hawk nose, the clean jawline and the thick jet-black hair. But his eyes weren't a warm, rich brown, they were an icy pale green, and he had a lean fitness about him that was possessed by very few Greek men in their early thirties, which Sadie estimated he must be.

Sadie saw him look at her and then frown slightly, leaning closer to her and very deliberately sniffing the air. The disparaging look he gave her made her whole body burn.

'That's an unusual perfume you're wearing. Is it up

for sale as well?' he demanded, in a voice that was pure soft sensuality with an accent that was equally pure Australian.

Sadie had had enough. In fact she'd had more than enough. Jerking back from him, she hissed bitingly, 'How dare you imply that I am for sale? What is it about men like you?'

'Men like me?' His pale green eyes narrowed icily. 'Well, let's put it this way—when it comes to women like you, then men like me tend to be a bit on the fussy side. I like my women like my perfume. Exclusive!'

He broke off suddenly, turning away from Sadie as the older man at his side touched his arm, and murmured something to him whilst looking at Sadie with distaste.

CHAPTER ONE

"Hubble bubble toil and trouble."

Sadie grinned as she met the teasing look her best friend Mary gave her as she stepped into the workroom where Sadie distilled the ingredients of her perfumes.

'Mmm... What a wonderful smell!' Mary exclaimed enthusiastically.

Sadie's smile widened. 'It's a special personal order I'm doing.'

'For someone famous? Who?' Mary pounced.

Sadie shook her head and laughed.

'You know I can't tell you that. It's a matter of client confidentiality.'

'Mmm...well, since the press got wind of the fact that a certain very, very famous singer has asked you to design a special signature scent for her, I can only assume...'

'Don't ask me any more questions about it,' Sadie begged fervently. Her smile changing to a look of concern. No doubt other people in her position would have welcomed the publicity she had received when it had become public knowledge that she had been asked to design the singer's perfume, but Sadie valued her privacy and her anonymity. And besides...

'I take it that you're still going to France?' Mary asked her.

Sadie's frown deepened.

'I don't have any real choice,' she admitted tersely, 'Raoul is making it impossible for me not to go. He's determined to sell the business to this Greek billionaire who wants to add it to his luxury goods consortium...'

'Leoneadis Stapinopolous, you mean?'

'Yes,' Sadie agreed even more shortly. 'Or the Greek Destroyer, as I call him!'

'Destroyer?' Mary shook her head. 'You really don't like him, do you?'

'I certainly don't like what he's planning to do to Francine!' Sadie told her fiercely.

'Well, by all accounts he's a very shrewd operator,' Mary allowed. 'The consortium he heads is worth billions, and since he took on that new designer to redesign the women's wear side of his acquisitions...well, there isn't a woman going who doesn't secretly yearn for a little something with their label on it.'

'No?' Sadie gave her a grim look. 'Well, I certainly don't.' When she saw her friend's face, she protested, 'Mary, he doesn't just want to buy the perfume house, he wants to buy the rights to the perfume my grandmother left to me as well.... Raoul is trying to pressurise me into selling it, but there is no way I am going to. That perfume was designed by my great-grandfather for my great-grandmother. He only allowed a handful of clients to have the perfume. My grandmother left the secret of its make-up to me because she knew that I would protect it! The whole reason she quarrelled with her brother was because he wanted to do exactly what Raoul wants to do now.'

'So don't go to France, then!' Mary told her forthrightly.

'I have to. I own thirty per cent of the business, and there's no way I'm going to let Raoul sell it to this... this...Greek...'

'Sex god?' Mary supplied helpfully, with a gleam in her eyes.

'Sex god?' Sadie queried disapprovingly.

'Haven't you seen his photo in the financial press?'

When Sadie shook her head Mary grinned.

'Wow, is he something else! His great-grandparents were Greek, and they settled in Australia as a young couple.'

'You seem to know a lot about him,' Sadie challenged her.

'Like I just said, he's a very sexy man—and I'm a sexy-man-hungry woman!' Mary grinned. 'Speaking of which, you are crazy, you know, hiding yourself away down here in Pembroke when you could be living the high life in Paris and Cannes—not to mention flying here, there and everywhere mixing powerfully potent perfumes for your celeb clients. How does Raoul feel about your business, by the way?' she asked.

'Francine no longer makes one-off perfumes to order,' Sadie responded, 'so there is no conflict of interest there. But...'

When she paused, Mary urged her to continue. 'But?'

Sadie gave a small sigh.

'Well, Raoul is pressing me to produce a new perfume. The one he tricked me into wearing at the trade fair was one of his late father's ''mistakes''. Grandmère always said her brother did not have a ''nose'', and her nephew seems to lack one also! Now he wants me to create a new perfume for Francine.'

'But you don't want to?' Mary guessed.

Sadie gave an exasperated sigh.

'I do want to. I want to very much. In fact it would be a dream come true for me to create a new Francine perfume. But...' Sadie lifted her hands expressively.

'As you know, my perfumes come from wholly natural materials, and are made in a traditional way, whereas Raoul favours modern procedures and chemically manufactured products. And it's not just that! I just hope that I can persuade him not to go ahead with this sale, Mary. Raoul is the majority shareholder, of course, but we are one of the last few remaining traditional perfume houses, and to sell our birthright for—'

'A mess of pottage?' Mary interrupted obligingly, tongue in cheek.

'I just don't want to sell the business to this Greek billionaire, and I have said as much to Raoul.'

'Mmm. All this talk of potions and lotions reminds me—how about mixing up a little something special and man-attracting for me?'

'I make perfume, not magic potions,' Sadie reminded her sternly.

Mary gave her a wicked look.

'Same thing, isn't it?' Her expression changed when she saw how sombre Sadie was looking. 'Something else is worrying you, isn't it?' she guessed.

Sadie frowned.

'Everything is so complicated, Mary. As it stands now Francine is worth very little in financial terms. The business is almost all dried up, and the staff are mainly freelancers. In reality all that is left is the name. And it is the name that this Greek Destroyer wants to buy.'

'Just the name?'

'I don't know! Raoul rang me last night and told me that he has informed Leoneadis Stapinopolous that I am working on a new scent, and that my scent and my skills will be part of the deal. I told him that he had no right to say any such thing. I am a minor shareholder in Francine, that is all. I do not work for the house!'

Angrily Sadie paced the floor.

'Raoul accused me of being deliberately difficult and of not realising what a wonderful opportunity this sale is. But an opportunity for what, Mary? Granted, it will give us both a considerable sum of money—especially Raoul, since he is the majority shareholder. But it will destroy the true essence of Francine and I just cannot agree to that. Never mind create a new scent. Raoul is putting so much pressure on me, though…'

She gave Mary a wry smile. 'If I do what Raoul wants me to do I shall be selling my birthright and my creative soul! Raoul reminded me last night that I was very fortunate to have been left the formula for Francine's most famous perfume by my grandmother. In actual fact he made me feel a little bit guilty about it, Mary.'

'Guilty? You? What on earth have you to feel guilty about?' Mary demanded robustly. 'Sadie, I know strictly speaking it is none of my business, but we have been friends for a long time and I just think that you should perhaps be a little bit cautious where your cousin is concerned,' she added forthrightly.

Sadie smiled in pleasure as she stepped into the foyer of her hotel. She had booked it on the recommendation of a client, who had raved about it to her, and now she could see why!

Although its location in Mougins meant that it was some distance away from Grasse, which was where the tall narrow house which was home to both the business headquarters and her cousin Raoul were situated, Sadie did not mind.

The hotel-cum-spa was the kind of place she loved—it was a positive haven of tranquillity and charm, unlike the glitzy Cannes hotels favoured by Raoul, who had been openly angry and bitter when he had told Sadie how much he resented the fact that the Paris premises the family had once owned were no longer in their possession.

'Why the hell did our great-grandfather choose to sell the Paris house and retain the one in Grasse? When I think what that Paris place would have been worth now!'

Sadie had said nothing. Her own grandmother had told her that the elegant family apartment and shop the family had originally owned in the capital had had to be sold in order to pay off her brother's gambling debts, and Sadie had no desire to reopen old family wounds!

She had booked into her hotel for the whole week, having decided to combine her business meeting with Raoul with visits to the flower-growers in the area from whom she sourced some of her supplies of natural ingredients for the perfumes she made.

As she checked in and signed the visitors' book Sadie hid a small smile as she saw the elegant French woman behind the reception desk sniff discreetly in her direction. The perfume Sadie was wearing was unique, and one she had steadfastly refused to supply to anyone else, no matter how much they pleaded with her to do so.

It was based on the original secret recipe her grandmother had left her, but with a subtle addition that was Sadie's own, which lightened its original heaviness just enough to make sure that it wasn't in any way oppressive and at the same time enhanced and echoed the scent of Sadie's own skin. It was Sadie's own favourite creation, her very personal signature scent, and she knew without false vanity that it was a perfume that—if she had wished to—she could have sold over and over again.

In its bottle the perfume always reminded her of her

grandmother; on her own body it was entirely and uniquely her.

The instructions she was given by the hotel receptionist took her to a low complex of rooms separate from the main building, set close to the adjoining spa block.

Her room itself was everything she had hoped it would be—luxuriously comfortable, elegantly simple and totally peaceful and private.

She had just enough time to unpack and change before she had to make her way to Grasse to meet Raoul, so that they could talk through her objections to his plans to sell the business to Leoneadis Stapinopolous—or the Greek Destroyer. Her mouth curled a little disdainfully as she reflected on the billionaire's motives for wanting to acquire Francine.

He would no doubt have seen that several of his competitors in the high-stratosphere business world they all occupied had already recognised the financial advantages that came with marketing a successful perfume—especially in today's climate, when so many women wanted to follow the example of actresses and models who had expressed their preference not for a modern perfume but instead for one of the rare and exclusive signature perfumes of the traditional perfume houses.

Her disdain changed to a frown, and she paused in the act of pulling on a comfortable pair of jeans. Formal business clothes were not really her thing, and after all this was not a formal business meeting, simply a discussion with her cousin and co-shareholder.

Francine had once produced some of the most coveted scents of its time, but Sadie knew that her grandmother's brother—Raoul's grandfather—had sold off the rights to virtually all of those scents, using the money to finance a series of disastrous business ventures and settle his gambling debts.

Today the only scents of any note Francine still produced were an old-fashioned lavender water and a 'gentleman's' pomade—neither of which, in her opinion, did the name of Francine any favours. For Sadie, the fascination and inspiration of working with old scent was in sourcing the necessary raw materials—some of which were no longer available to modern-day perfume makers, for reasons of ecology and for reasons of economy, in that many of those who grew the flowers needed for their work had switched from traditional to modern methods of doing so.

Sadie considered herself very fortunate in having found a family close to Grasse who not only still grew roses and jasmine for the perfume industry in the old-fashioned labour-intensive way, but who also operated their own traditional distillery. The Lafount family produced rose absolute and jasmine absolute of the highest quality, and Sadie knew she was very privileged to be able to buy her raw materials from them.

Both in their seventies now, Pierre Lafount and his brother Henri actually remembered her own grandmother, and delighted Sadie with their stories of how they could remember seeing her when she had visited the growing fields and the distillery with her own father. The Lafount family's rose and jasmine absolutes were highly sought after, and Sadie knew that it was primarily because of their affection for her grandmother that they allowed her to buy from them in such small quantities.

'Virtually all that we produce is pre-sold under contract to certain long-standing customers,' they had told Sadie—from which she had understood that those customers would be the most famous and respected of the

established perfume houses. 'But there is a little to spare
and we shall make that available to you,' they had added
magnanimously

Raoul, typically, had laughed at Sadie for what he
called her sentimentality.

'You're crazy,' he had said to her, shaking his head in
disbelief. 'Paying heaven alone knows what for their
stuff, when it can be manufactured in a lab at a fraction
of the cost.'

'But that is the whole point, Raoul,' Sadie had told
him dryly. 'The essence of the scents I want to create
cannot be manufactured.'

Raoul had shrugged dismissively. 'Who can tell the
difference?'

'I can!' Sadie had answered calmly.

And now apparently Raoul wanted to sell Francine to
someone who was as ignorant and uncaring of what real
scent was all about as he was. Well, not if she had anything to do with it, he wasn't, Sadie decided stubbornly.

As she went to the parking area to collect her hire car
Sadie noticed a frenzy of anxious activity surrounding
the presence of a huge Mercedes limousine, with its windows blacked out. But she had too much on her mind to
do any more than give both the vehicle and its entourage
of anxious attendants a wryly amused glance as she
skirted past them.

Spring was quite definitely on the way, Sadie acknowledged as she sniffed the air appreciatively. The scent of
mimosa was heavenly!

She knew the way to Grasse almost as well as she
knew the history of Francine and although modern mo-
torways and roads had altered things since her grandmother's time, Sadie suspected that just from listening

over and over again to her description of the place she could almost have found her away around the town blind-fold.

Her grandmother's childhood had been in her own words an idyllic and financially cocooned one; her father had adored and spoiled her, but then war had broken out and everything had changed. Sadie's great-grandfather had died and her grandmother had fled to England with the young English major she had fallen in love with.

The quarrel between her grandmother and her great-uncle had led to a rift which had never been healed, and stubbornly her grandmother had refused to return to Grasse. Maybe she never physically went back, but in her memories, her emotions and her heart she had returned over and over again, Sadie acknowledged as she eased her hire car down the narrow maze of streets crowded with historic buildings. Here and there she could see the now disused chimneys of what had once been the town's thriving perfume distilleries.

Other perfume houses had turned their work into a thriving tourist industry, but Francine remained as it had always done. The tall, narrow house guarding the privacy of a cobbled courtyard which lay behind its now slightly shabby façade, the paint flaking off its old-fashioned shutters and off the ancient solid wooden gates, beyond which lay the courtyard and a collection of outbuildings, linked together with covered galleries and walkways, in which Francine perfumes had traditionally been made.

Had *always* been made! Sadie frowned as she swerved expertly across the path of a battered old Citroen, ignoring the infuriated gestures and horn of its irate driver, swinging her hire car neatly into the single available parking space on the piece of empty land across the road from the house.

If Raoul had his way, and Francine was sold to the
Greek Destroyer, then the manufacture of its perfumes
would be transferred to a modern venue and produced
with synthetic materials, its remaining few permanent elderly employees summarily retired and their skills lost.

Hélène, Raoul's ancient and unfriendly housekeeper,
opened the door to Sadie's knock, her face set in its normal expression of dour misanthropy.

The few brave beams of sunlight which had managed
to force their way through the grimy narrow windows
highlighted golden squares of dust on the old-fashioned
furniture in the stone-floored entrance hall. It made
Sadie's artistic soul ache not just to see the neglect, but
also the wasted opportunity to create something beautiful
in this old and unloved historic house.

The rear door that opened out into the courtyard was
half open, and through it Sadie could see the cobbled
yard and hear the tinkle of water falling from a small
fountain into the shallow stone basin beneath it. A
lavender-flowered wisteria clothed the back wall of the
courtyard, and a thin tabby cat lay washing its paws beneath it in a patch of warm sunshine.

Instinctively Sadie hesitated, drawn to the courtyard
and its history, the memories it held of her ancestors and
their creations. Its air—unlike that of the house, which
smelled of dust and neglect—held a heady fusion of everything that Sadie loved best.

Hélène was growing impatient and glowering at her.

Reluctantly Sadie turned away from the courtyard and
headed for the stairs that led up to the house's living
quarters and Raoul's 'office'.

Hélène, who protected her employer as devotedly as
any guard dog, preceded Sadie up the stairs, giving her
a final suspicious look before pushing open the door.

Ready for the battle she knew was about to commence, Sadie took a deep breath and stepped firmly into the room, beginning calmly, 'Raoul, I am not—'

Abruptly she stopped in mid-sentence, her eyes widening, betraying her, as shock coursed through her, scattering her carefully assembled thoughts like a small whirlwind.

There, right in front of her, standing framed in the window of Raoul's office, was…was…

CHAPTER TWO

SADIE gulped and struggled to regain her equilibrium and self-control, but those perma frost eyes were trapping her in an invisible web of subtle power.

His gaze made her feel dizzy, disorientated, helplessly enmeshed in sensations and emotions that terrified her into fierce, self-protective and angry hostility. And yet at the same time beneath all those feelings lay another, stronger, and darker one too. A rush of instinctive awareness of her vulnerability towards him as a man who, at the deepest most intense level of herself, she was responsive to.

She could feel her body quickening like mercury just because he was there, her every single sense reacting not just to the sight of him but to everything else as well, including his scent, male, potent and dangerous, prickling her sensitive nose, making her want to both breathe in the essence of him and yet at the same time close herself off from it and from him. Instinctively Sadie tensed against what she was experiencing, her eyes liquid gold with the intensity of her feelings.

She gave a small inward shudder.

'I warned you, didn't I, Leon, that my cousin doesn't exactly present a businesslike image?' Sadie could hear Raoul saying.

Leon? Leoneadis Stapinopolous? The Greek Destroyer? Silver spears of hostility and wariness glinted in the gold of Sadie's gaze as she stared at him.

'Miss Roberts.' A brief inclination of his head, an

Olympian acknowledgement of her presence which matched the unimpressed Australian scorch of his voice.

'Okay, Sadie, now that you're here let's get down to business. Leon doesn't have much time,' Raoul breezed on.

So he had no time and too much money. It was a dangerously volatile combination—much like the man himself, Sadie reflected inwardly. He hadn't, she noticed, made any attempt to shake hands with her, for which she was mightily thankful, as the last thing she wanted or needed right now was any kind of physical contact with him.

He had made no indication of having recognised her from the trade fair. Perhaps he had not done so. Maybe, unlike her, he had not suffered that feral surge of instant recognition. Maybe? There was no maybe about it! He was a man who was armoured against any kind of emotional vulnerability!

As Raoul started to talk expansively about the benefits which would accrue to them all on Leon's acquisition of Francine Sadie had to force herself to focus on what he was saying. Deliberately she started to turn away from Leon to face her cousin, hoping that by doing so she could lessen the almost mesmerising effect Leon's presence was having on her.

She spun round on her heel and a flurry of dust motes danced around her. Out of the corner of her eye she just caught the swift movement Leon made as he stepped towards her, his fingers curling round her upper arm, shackling her. She could feel the pulse throbbing at the base of her throat, driven by the acute intensity of the sensations bombarding her—the cool, steely grip of his hand on her arm, the sleek suppleness of his fingers, hard and strong, the dry, controlled warmth of his flesh, the steadiness of the surge of his blood in his veins as her own pounding heartbeat went wild.

Instinctively Sadie's head snapped round. Her eyes were on a level with his throat. A drenching surge of hot female awareness roared over her, swamping her. She wasn't used to feeling like this, reacting like this, wanting like this, she acknowledged shakily.

Wanting... How could she want him? He was a stranger, her enemy, representative of everything she disliked and despised.

He was leaning towards her, his cold gaze releasing her as his eyelids came down, shuttering his eyes away from her as his head slanted towards her throat.

It was impossible for her to stop the fierce tremor that raced through her as she felt the warmth of his breath against her skin

'Well, at least the scent you are wearing today is a great improvement on whatever it was you were touting at the trade fair.'

His hold on her upper arm slackened the imprisoning bracelet of hard male flesh, his hand sliding smoothly down to her wrist and then holding it whilst the soft pad of his thumb pressed deliberately against her frantically jumping pulse. The shuttered lids lifted. Shockingly, the ice had melted and turned into a shimmering blinding heat that sent her heartbeat into overdrive.

'What is it?'

What was it? Didn't he know? Couldn't he tell?

'It's obviously a very highly marketable scent, and...'

Scent; he was talking about her perfume! *Her* perfume, Sadie reminded herself savagely as she pulled herself free and stepped back from him.

'Pity you didn't choose to wear it at the trade fair. What you did wear—'

'Was Raoul's father's creation and had nothing to do with me,' Sadie snapped sharply, quickly defending her own professional status. 'I didn't even want to wear it!'

'I should hope not,' Leon agreed suavely. 'Not with your reputation.' He gave her a silkily intimidating look. 'One of the reasons we are prepared to pay so generously for Francine is, as I am sure you must know, so that we can secure the combination of its old recipes and your perfumery skills. We want to bring to the market a new perfume under the Francine name which...'

The briskness of his manner snapped Sadie back to reality. This man was her enemy—bent on destroying everything she held dear professionally—and she had better keep that thought right to the forefront of her mind! Accusingly she looked at Raoul.

'Raoul, I think—' she began.

Raoul stopped her, smiling fawningly at the other man. 'Leon, Sadie is as excited about your plans for Francine as I am myself—'

'No, I am not,' Sadie interrupted him sharply. 'You know my views on this subject, Raoul,' she reminded her cousin. 'And you assured me that we would have time to talk in private today, before we met with...with anyone else!'

What was the matter with her? Why was she finding it so hard to so much as say his name without betraying the effect he was having on her?

'Raoul may know your opinions,' Leon cut in smoothly, 'but since I do not, perhaps you would be good enough to run them past me.'

'Sadie—' Raoul began warningly, but Sadie had no intention of listening to him, and refused to be intimidated by the challenge she could see gleaming dangerously in Leon's eyes.

Leon was no longer the man whose presence had swamped her female defences, the man who had somehow reached out to her and touched her senses and her emotions at their most primeval level. Instead he was the man who was threatening everything that mattered most to her. And there was no way that Sadie would break the mental promise she had made to her grandmother that she would cherish and protect the inheritance she had passed on to her in every way that she could.

Turning to confront Leon, Sadie began as calmly as she could. 'I may only be a minority shareholder in the business, but I do own one-third of the shares.'

'And I own two-thirds, 'Raoul reminded her angrily. 'If I want to sell the business to Leon, then as the majority shareholder—'

'The business maybe, Raoul.' Sadie stopped him, her face beginning to turn pink with the force of her emotions. 'But—'

'I am not really interested in which one of you has the majority shareholding in the business,' Leon cut in grimly. 'What I and my shareholders are interested in is the reintroduction of Francine's most famous scent and the addition of an equally successful new creation! Using modern production methods—'

'I will never create a perfume made in such a way!' Sadie told him passionately. 'To me, synthetic scents are an abhorrence. They are a mockery of everything a true scent should be. A great fragrance can only be made from natural ingredients. It does not just reflect its origins, it also reflects and highlights the…certain essential properties of its wearer…'

'Certain properties?' The dark eyebrows rose mockingly. 'You mean it reflects and highlights a woman's sensuality?'

To her disgust, Sadie realised that she was actually blushing!

'Sadie, you are totally out of step with what's happening today in the perfume business,' Raoul objected angrily.

'No, Raoul,' Sadie argued back, glad to have an excuse to turn away from Leon and focus on her cousin instead. 'You are the one who is out of step. The mass perfume market may still be governed by chemically produced products, but at the top end of the market there is an increasing demand for traditionally produced perfumes. If either of you two had done your homework you would both know this,' Sadie told them fiercely. 'And the fact that you do not know it, the fact that you have not done your homework, makes me have very serious doubts about the ultimate success of any new product you might launch.'

Whilst Raoul was beginning to bluster an angry protest, it was Leon's reaction that interested her more, Sadie acknowledged. His mouth had tightened into a hard line and he was frowning at her.

'Mass-market perfume is big business,' he told her harshly. 'The production of a perfume which can only be afforded by a few élite buyers does not interest me.'

'Well, it should,' Sadie countered. 'Because it is the scent worn by the élite buyers that the mass-market buyers most want to wear themselves. And why shouldn't they aspire to do so? Why should they be fobbed off with a synthetic substitute that is never going to come anywhere near equating to the real thing?'

'Perhaps because the synthetic substitute is affordable and the real thing is not,' Leon told her pungently.

'You say that, but it could be!' Sadie claimed immediately. 'It is perfectly feasible for high-quality natural perfumes to be made at a reasonable cost. But of course the profit margin on them would be much smaller, and that is the real reason why big business like you refuse to produce them. Because profit is all that matters to you. You and men like you are as...as soulless as...as...synthetic perfume!' Sadie told him passionately.

'Is that a fact?'

The silky tone of Leon's voice made Sadie quiver inwardly with wariness, but she refused to heed her body's own protective warning, eyeing Leon defiantly.

'Well, you, of course, would be in a perfect position to judge me, wouldn't you? Having met me how often? Twice?'

'Three times,' Sadie corrected him, and then felt her body burn with self-conscious heat as he looked thoughtfully at her.

'Three times?'

'How many times I've seen you is an irrelevance.' Sadie overrode him.

'The world's opinion of the status of the corporation you run and its aims and beliefs are written about publicly and frequently in the financial press, and—'

'The financial press?' Leon stopped her. 'They report company and corporation policy. They do not make it,' he told her acidly.

'I don't care what you say,' Sadie protested emotionally. 'Raoul already knows my views on his plans to sell Francine to you—against my wishes. In fact I came here hoping that I might be able to dissuade him, but I can see that there is no hope of that! I cannot stop him from selling to you, since he is the majority shareholder, but there is no way that I would ever—ever...prostitute my...my gift of a good ''nose'' for perfume by selling that to you!'

Abruptly Sadie realised how silent both men had become. Raoul was looking angry and embarrassed, whilst Leon...

The chill was back in his green eyes, but strangely now there was a glow beneath it, a glitter like the beginning of the Northern lights on ice, all white fire shimmer and danger, a warning of a strength and a power that secretly she already felt vulnerably in awe of.

Which was all the more reason why she should not give in to him, Sadie told herself militantly.

'Stirring words. Pity they don't seem to have been matched by your actions!'

Leon's cool words were every bit as chillingly dangerous as the look he had given her. Outraged, Sadie turned to look to Raoul for support, but her cousin was out of earshot on the other side of the room, searching through some papers on his desk.

Leaning closer to her, Leon continued with steely venom, 'When I saw you at the trade fair it was quite obvious that you were—'

'That was Raoul's idea,' Sadie protested defensively.

'Raoul's idea, Francine's perfume—and your body. As a matter of interest, what kind of response, other than the obvious, did that cheap sideshow you were putting on generate? I am, of course, asking about the amount of sales it generated, and not the number of offers you received for your body!'

Sadie glared at him.

'How dare you say that? I had no idea that men would assume I was also available.' Her mouth compressed with anger whilst her face burned hotly with sharply remembered shame.

'No idea?' The contempt in his eyes left her sensitivities burned raw. 'Oh, come on. You can't expect me to believe that! You paraded yourself openly and deliberately, wearing—'

Sadie had had enough.

'I was perfectly respectably dressed, and if I'd had any idea that what I had assumed to be a collection of professional businessmen would behave like…like a pack of…of…animals, I would never, ever have allowed Raoul to persuade me into helping him.'

How could her cousin even think of selling Francine to this man? To this…this monster?

With a change of tack so swift and unexpected that it caught her totally off guard, Leon demanded, 'That scent you're wearing today—what is it?'

Immediately Sadie tilted her chin and eyed him defiantly.

'It's a perfume of my own.'

'I like it,' Leon told her crisply. 'Indeed, I should have thought that it would be a highly marketable addition to the Francine name. In fact, I am surprised that you are not already marketing it!'

Anger flashed in Sadie's eyes, turning them as brilliant a gold as the sun streaming in through the dusty windows.

'This scent was created by me for my own personal use.'

'It's an original formula of your own devising?'

Sadie frowned. Why was he asking her so many questions? He was beginning to seriously annoy her!

'Not exactly,' she admitted haughtily. 'It's actually based on a one-time famous Francine perfume called Myrrh.'

Sadie stopped speaking as the dark eyebrows snapped together and she was treated to a frowning look.

'Myrrh…I see!'

In the warning-packed silence that followed Sadie could feel her nerve-ends tightening.

'Aren't I right in thinking that that was Francine's most exclusive and successful scent?' Leon asked smoothly.

Now it was Sadie's turn to frown.

'Yes, it was,' she acknowledged. 'You have done your research well,' she admitted, unable to resist adding a little acidly, 'Or rather someone has.'

No doubt a man like him paid other people to provide him with whatever information he needed! He could certainly afford to do so, after all!

'You say that the scent you are wearing is based on Francine's Myrrh? I am surprised that you allowed Sadie to tamper with something so valuable and irreplaceable, Raoul,' he announced to Raoul, looking over Sadie's head towards her cousin.

Infuriated as much by his manner as his words, it gave Sadie a great deal of satisfaction to tell him coldly, 'Actually, Raoul has no power to "allow" anyone to do a thing with the original Myrrh formula, since her father left it to my grandmother and she left it to me! A fact which I'm sure Raoul intended to share with you in the near future.'

Sadie saw immediately that Leon had not been told that she owned the Myrrh formula. He looked at her, his mouth thinning, before turning and demanding, 'So you own one-third of Francine and the Myrrh formula?'

'Yes,' Sadie confirmed emphatically, with a great deal of satisfaction.

'This is a matter I shall need to discuss with my lawyers. The Myrrh name, in my opinion, belongs to Francine, and—'

'And the Myrrh scent belongs to me,' Sadie informed him angrily. 'If you think that you are going to browbeat and bully me with threats of lawyers, then let me tell you that you cannot. I'm going, Raoul,' she told her cousin shortly. 'I've wasted enough time here!'

'Sadie—' Raoul began to protest, but Sadie ignored him, crossing the room and pulling open the heavy door.

Her visit, Sadie acknowledged bitterly as she got back to her car, had been a complete waste—not just of her time, but more importantly of her hope and her desire to somehow persuade Raoul not to sell the business.

She attempted to soothe her spirits and her senses by walking through the old town, along the narrow streets that wound between wonderful old seventeenth- and eighteenth-century buildings, pausing to glance in shop windows before stepping out of the sunlight into the shadows until she had finally made her leisurely way to the principal square at the top of the old town.

The Place aux Aires housed a daily market of fresh flowers and regional foods. However, it was so late in the day that the flowers and food had all been sold by now, and the stallholders were packing up for the day. She decided to find a café in the arcade that lined one long side of the square and drink a cup of coffee whilst she admired the pretty three-tiered fountain which graced the square.

Down below where she had parked she could see the empty shell of one of the town's old distilleries, neglected and unused now, in these modern times—thanks to men like Leon! Before getting into her car something made her stop and look up towards the window to Raoul's office.

Her whole body stiffened as she saw Leon standing there, looking down at her.

Angrily she held his gaze, determined not to be the

first one to look away, her concentration only broken when another driver, anxious for her to vacate her parking spot, beeped his horn to attract her attention.

In the dusty silence of the room the two men looked at one another.

'Look, Leon,' Raoul began breezily, 'I know what you must be thinking, but I promise you that everything will be fine. I'll talk to her. She'll come round. You'll see. Of course it would help if you were a bit more, well…friendly towards her! The woman hasn't been born who doesn't respond to a bit of coaxing and flattery,' Raoul told him.

Silently Leon studied him before saying gently, 'Friendly? Well, I assume that you know your cousin far better than I do, Raoul. Although I wouldn't have thought…'

'Oh, Sadie is okay.' Raoul gave a small shrug. 'Of course, she's had her own way all her life—been spoiled and indulged. Her grandmother saw to that! She married into a wealthy English family.'

He gave another dismissive shrug, neglecting to add that that wealth had been lost long before Sadie's birth!

'There's nothing to worry about, Leon,' Raoul continued confidently. 'Sadie's a bit naïve. She gets all fired up and on her high horse, all moralistic at times, that's all. I put it down to the fact that she was virtually brought up by her grandmother! Sadie's a bit old-fashioned, if you know what I mean, but I can soon talk her round! She's just not had much to do with men, of course— thanks to her grandmother.'

'Oh, yes, that would explain it,' Leon murmured suavely, but Raoul was oblivious to his sarcasm.

'Leave everything to me, Leon!' he continued arrogantly.

Leon frowned. It was becoming increasingly obvious to him that Sadie was in a very vulnerable position where Raoul and the business were concerned. Had she been a member of *his* family… But of course she was not, and there was no way he could afford to let his Greek ancestry urge him into the self-elected role of protective paterfamilias towards her! Indeed, there was no reason why he should concern himself about her in any way—not after the open hostility she had shown him!

His frown deepened. Hostility wasn't something Leon was used to women exhibiting towards him. Quite the opposite. There had never been a woman he had needed to pursue, and he certainly wasn't going to start chasing one who had made it plain that she didn't want him! Of course he wasn't! No, all he felt was pique and chagrin; these were emotions so unimportant that he wasn't even going to bother acknowledging them, never mind responding to them!

What *was* important—almost vital—was securing the acquisition of Francine. Leon had understood from Raoul when they had first discussed the matter that in acquiring Francine he would also be acquiring its existing scent formulae, including that for Myrrh, and the perfume-creating skills of Sadie herself. Now it seemed that Raoul had not been entirely honest with him.

'Everything will be fine, Leon. I promise you,' Raoul repeated insistently. 'All we need to do is convince Sadie that you'll let her use her precious natural ingredients and she'll be eating out of your hand and begging you to let her concoct a new perfume for you.'

'I'm afraid that isn't an option, Raoul. The cost alone of simply acquiring natural raw products would give my board a collective heart attack! It just isn't commercially viable to produce a mass-market scent by traditional methods.'

'Well, maybe not. But you don't have to tell her that, do you?' Raoul challenged him.

'Are you suggesting that I should deliberately lie to her?'

'You want the Myrrh formula and you want her to work for you, don't you?' Raoul asked him shrewdly.

Leon looked away from him briefly before demanding curtly, 'Raoul, why wasn't I informed about your cousin's views—and, more specifically, that she owned the formula for Myrrh?'

Raoul gave a dismissive shrug

'I didn't think it was that important. You only asked me for a list of the perfumes my father had sold off. Anyway, like you, I am sure you could prove that legally the formula really belongs to the business. After all, a man with your resources can afford the very best of law-yers—lawyers who can prove anything. Sadie hasn't the money to take you on in court, but of course it will save you a lot of fuss if she gives in and hands it over to you—and I promise you that if you play it my way she will!'

'You seem remarkably unconcerned about your cousin, if I may say so,' Leon commented dryly.

Carelessly, and without any trace of embarrassment, Raoul told him, 'Certainly I am not as concerned for her as I am for myself. Why should I be? We've only been in contact for the last few months. I need to sell Francine, Leon. If not to you then to someone else. And there is no way I am going to let Sadie or anyone else interfere with that.'

'I think I'd prefer to speak with your cousin myself,'

Leon announced coolly, adding warningly, 'It's true that I want Sadie's expertise, and that I want the Myrrh formula, but there's no way I would agree to her being deceived about my future plans for the business. I'm afraid that in my book honesty can never be sacrificed for expediency!'

Initially, when he had seen Sadie at the trade fair, Leon had assumed that she was made much in the same mould as her cousin. But now he wasn't nearly so sure.

But he could not afford the luxury of sympathy, Leon warned himself, and unless he had misjudged her Sadie would certainly not welcome receiving it from him.

Raoul gave a careless shrug.

'Fine—if that's what you want to do. After all, you're going to be the boss!'

Going to be, but was not as yet, Raoul reminded himself angrily after Leon had gone.

There was no way he was going to allow Sadie to mess up this deal for him, and no way he was going to risk leaving it to Leon to persuade his cousin to change her mind. Not when Raoul knew that he could do so much more easily and quickly.

In the privacy of his elegant hotel suite, Leon completed the telephone conversation he had been having with his chief executive in Sydney and then went to stand in front of the large window that opened out onto his private balcony.

Sadie's ownership of the Myrrh formula was a complication he had not anticipated, as was Sadie herself. But he had no intention of using Raoul's suggested underhand tactics to rectify it! Underhandedness and deceit were weapons of engagement that were never employed in the Stapinopolous business empire—even though once they had been used against it to devastating and almost totally destructive effect.

Leon's expression hardened. Those dark years when his family had almost lost the business were behind them now, but they had left their mark on him. However, right now it wasn't the past he was thinking about so much as...

A little grimly Leon acknowledged that he wasn't sure which had distracted him the most—the tantalising length of Sadie's slim legs encased in the jeans she had been wearing, or the intensity with which her eyes had reflected her every emotion.

She was, he decided grimly, impossibly stubborn, fiercely passionate and hopelessly idealistic. She was a go-it-aloner, a renegade from the conventional business and profit-focused world of modern perfumes. She was, in short, trouble every which way there was. A zealot, a would-be prophet, intent on stirring up all kinds of disorder and destined to cause chaos!

She would make his board of directors shake in their corporate shoes and question his financial judgement for even thinking about wanting to get involved in a business in which she played even the smallest part.

Did she really believe that it was feasible to produce what amounted to a handmade scent in the quantities needed to satisfy a mass-market appetite at an affordable price, using old-fashioned methods and natural raw materials?

He was already facing opposition from some members of his board over his plans to acquire Francine—but it was an opposition he fully intended to quash! An opposition he *had* to quash if he was not to find himself in danger of being voted off his own board!

'Why Francine?' one of his co-directors had demanded

belligerently. 'Hell, Leon, there are dozens of other perfume houses in far better financial condition, with more assets, and—'

'It is precisely because Francine is Francine that I want it,' Leon had countered coolly. 'The name has a certain resonance. An allure. And because of its current run-down state we can acquire it at a reasonable cost and build up a completely new profile for it. The new Francine perfume, when it comes on the market, is going to be *the* perfume to wear.'

'The new Francine perfume?' one of the others had questioned. 'Hell, Leon, if there's to be a new perfume why buy the damned outfit at all? Why not just get some chemist to come up with a new perfume for us and get some actress or model to front it for us? That's what everyone else is doing.'

'Which is exactly why it is not going to be what we shall do,' Leon had responded briskly.

He was taking a very big gamble. He knew that. For every classic fragrance there were a hundred perfumes that had been forgotten, buried in obscurity. Leon wasn't a fool. He knew that he had his detractors and his enemies in the shark-infested waters of the business world in which he lived; he knew too that there were also those who were simply plain jealous of his success. And all of them, whatever their motivation, would enjoy seeing him fail and fall.

Launching a new perfume was always a risk, even for a well-established perfume house with a stable of existing popular products. All Francine had was a name and a couple of old-fashioned formulae.

A couple, but not Myrrh, it now seemed.

Broodingly, Leon turned his back on the view. On the bedside table amongst his personal possessions was a small framed photograph. Going over to it, he picked it up and studied the delicately pretty feminine features of its subject, a sombre expression darkening his eyes.

The Sadies of this world didn't really know what life was all about. Handed a silver spoon at birth, they could take what they wanted from life as a right.

Was she really oblivious to the fact that only a small handful of women could afford the luxury of the kind of scents she blended? Or did she simply not care?

Well, he cared. He cared one hell of a lot—as she was about to discover!

As she drove past the flower fields belonging to Pierre, Sadie exhaled a deep breath of pleasure and satisfaction. Pleasure because both the sight and the scent of growing flowers always lifted her spirits, and satisfaction because she had the power to prevent the Greek Destroyer from wrecking the precious heritage her grandmother had passed on to her.

Pierre and his brother grew both jasmine and roses. A swift, delicate-fingered person could pick half a kilo of the jasmine blossoms in an hour, and the picked blossoms sold at a hefty price—as Sadie had good cause to know. The delicacy of the jasmine flower meant that it required year-round care by humans rather than machines. And in the rose fields stood the precious, wonderful Rose de Mai, from which the rose absolute which Sadie used in her perfumes was made.

Pierre and his wife Jeannette came hurrying out to the car to welcome Sadie, embracing her affectionately.

'So Francine is to be sold and soon you will be creating a fine new perfume for the new owners? That is excellent news. A talent such as yours should be recognised and allowed to truly shine. I am already looking forward to saying that I know the creator of the next classic scent,' Pierre announced teasingly, once Sadie was seated at the scrubbed kitchen table, drinking the coffee Jeannette had made for her.

Sadie frowned as she listened to him. She had expected Pierre to share her own feelings towards the sale of the business, instead of which he was making it plain that he thought it was an excellent opportunity for her.

'It is true that Leon…he…the would-be owner does wish me to create a new perfume—but, Pierre, he is only interested in mass-market perfumes made out of chemical ingredients,' Sadie objected.

Pierre shrugged. 'He is a businessman, as we all must be these days, and perhaps not totally *au fait* with the complexities of our business. He does not have your knowledge perhaps, *petite*. Therefore it is up to you, in the name and memory of your *grandmère*, to help him,' Pierre pronounced sagely.

'Help him!' Sadie's voice was a squeak of female outrage. 'I would rather—' she began, and then stopped as Pierre overrode her.

'But you must do so,' he said calmly. 'For if people like yourself do not give their knowledge and their expertise to those who are coming new into the business then how are we to go on? This is a wonderful opportunity for you Sadie!' Pierre repeated emphatically.

'It is?' Sadie stared at him whilst Pierre nodded his head in vigorous confirmation.

'Indeed it is, and your grandmother would be the first to say so if she were here. Ah, I can remember hearing her tell her father that she longed for the House of Francine to produce a new perfume—a fragrance which would rival that of the most famous perfumery.'

'You heard her say that?' Sadie swallowed the emotional lump which was suddenly blocking her throat. She had loved her grandmother so much, and she knew how much Francine had meant to her.

'You are indeed fortunate to have been given such an opportunity,' Pierre was telling her.

'I am?' Sadie struggled to marshal all the objections she had had no difficulty in hurling at Leon's head. 'But I prefer to work on a one-to-one basis with my clients,' she managed to point out.

'Pff…' Pierre gave a Gallic thrust of his shoulders. 'Filmstars and the like—they come and go and are as changeable and fickle as a mistral wind! They would quite happily take your perfume and claim it as their own creation if it suited them, and just as easily turn to someone else.'

A little reluctantly Sadie was forced to acknowledge that what he was saying had a grain of truth to it. Right now her own perfumes were very popular, but that could all change overnight. And if it did…

She frowned. What was she trying to tell herself? Surely she wasn't actually going to give in—to sell out— let Leon walk all over her?

But what if Pierre was right? What if she could create a wonderful new perfume—so wonderful and so popular that the whole world would want to wear it?

Sadie began to feel slightly dizzy, almost drugged with her own surging excitement, with the thought of fulfilling her grandmother's unexpectedly revealed dream.

But Sadie was no fool. She knew perfectly well that it was impossible to mass-produce a perfume created only out of natural ingredients, which meant…

'I can't do it, Pierre,' she told him, shaking her head. 'You know how I feel about synthetic scents.'

Pierre nodded. 'Indeed, we all feel the same, but these

are modern times and it is impossible to mass-produce a scent from natural materials alone. There has to be a compromise... But think of what a triumph it would be were you to create one based on a perfect combination of old and new, natural and synthetic.'

'No one has ever managed to do that,' Sadie objected.

'Until now,' Pierre told her slyly.

Giddily Sadie tried to clear her head.

'Do you really think that I can do it?' she asked Pierre shakily.

'Of a certainty! If not you, then who else? You have the history and the knowledge, the experience, the tenderness, the understanding... You have a gift and, like a truly exceptional perfume, it is only waiting to be released in order to charm everyone who experiences it!'

Sadie stared at him in bemusement. She felt as though she was riding a rollercoaster of emotions and thoughts. Could she do it? Could she create a perfume to rival that of the very greatest of houses?

She could almost see it in her mind's eye. She would call her perfume Francine.... It would have a similar base to Myrrh, but be a little lighter, delicate enough to make everyone who smelled it move closer to its wearer in order to breathe it again. It would be sensual and yet joyously teasing, flirtatious but still serious—a woman's perfume, passionate, charming, enticing... It would be a scent her grandmother would have been proud for her to create!

To her surprise, Sadie discovered that she was on her feet and halfway towards the kitchen door.

'I must go, Pierre,' she told him dizzily.

She would need to make sure that Leon knew she was not to be messed with, of course. And she'd make it clear that she must be given carte blanche where the creation of her scent was concerned. There was no way that Leon was going to overrule her or dictate to her, and she fully intended to make that plain to him. The scent would be her creation and would bear the Francine name. It would, Sadie decided, her heart singing, restore to the house of Francine its old status and glory. It would be her abiding gift of love to her grandmother!

CHAPTER THREE

SADIE picked up the telephone message Raoul had left, asking her to come back to Grasse so that they could talk, as she got into her car.

Still under the heady influence of listening to Pierre, she sent Raoul a text message informing him that she was on her way.

This time Raoul himself opened the door to her, hugging her warmly and apologising to her for their earlier quarrel before she could so much as say a single word.

'You promised me that we would be able to talk about selling the business before we met with Leon,' Sadie reminded him warily.

'I know, I know...' Raoul was all but wringing his hands as he ushered her solicitously into the salon.

It was such a shame that the house was so run-down and neglected, Sadie reflected for the second time that day. It had so much potential, and could in the right hands be turned into the most wonderful family home. Emotionally she looked out into the courtyard, trying to imagine her grandmother playing there as a little girl. But bemusingly, as the sunlight glittered on the droplets of water from the fountain, the child she suddenly visualised toddling across the ancient paved stones was not a miniature version of her grandmother but instead a sturdy, dark-haired green-eyed little boy, who looked shockingly like...

Her whole body heating in the sudden surge of recognition that burned through her, Sadie dragged her trapped gaze away from the courtyard. Why on earth had she imagined Leon's baby boy there? And, even more disturbing, why had she felt that unmistakable sharp maternal tug on her own heartstrings as she did so?

She did not want Leon's child. Why, the very thought was—

'Sadie? Come back! You aren't listening to me.'

There was a note of distinct peevishness in Raoul's voice. Guiltily Sadie turned round to look at him.

'I'm sorry. What were you saying?'

'I was just trying to tell you that after you left I had a long talk with Leon and explained to him that if he was serious about wanting to buy Francine and having you on board as well, then he was going to have to compromise on a few things.'

Sadie blinked as she listened to him.

'You did?' she exclaimed, unable to hide her astonishment. She had been expecting to hear Raoul verbally persuading her, if not actually bullying her into changing her mind.

'I did,' Raoul confirmed. 'I know you and I haven't always seen eye to eye over Francine, Sadie, but I have to say that, listening to you today, I began to realise that you were making some very valid points. And I have said as much to Leon.'

Her cousin's unexpected support was leaving Sadie momentarily lost for words.

'I...see...' she managed to say. 'And how did Leon react to that?'

'Well, at first, of course, he was reluctant to agree with me—and I'll be honest with you, Sadie, it took me a hell of a long time to bring him round to seeing my side of the argument. In the end I had to remind him that unless he wanted to alienate you completely he was just going to have to compromise…'

'I'm sure he loved that,' Sadie could not help murmuring dryly.

'Well, he is a businessman, after all, and he is now prepared to concede that if you agree to the sale, and provided you work for Francine, then he is prepared to allow you to base any new perfume you create on natural products.'

'Base?' Sadie queried cautiously, whilst her heart felt as though it was bouncing around inside her chest in excitement and relief.

Unbelievably, Raoul had taken her side, her part, and had managed to convince Leon that she was right!

'Well, you will have to negotiate with him to see how much of any new perfume can be natural products and how much chemically manufactured. And, of course, he will want access to the Myrrh formula.'

'Access, maybe—but I am not prepared to hand over ownership,' Sadie shot back immediately.

Raoul made no response, his expression suddenly becoming almost theatrically anxious.

'Sadie, I have not wanted to mention this. I do have my pride after all.' He looked away from her and rubbed his hand over his eyes. 'But I'm afraid that I haven't been entirely…honest with you about…about certain things.'

Sadie waited.

'The fact is that…well, I have got myself in a bit of a financial mess. And if I can't sell Francine to Leon then…'

'Then?' Sadie prompted him, dry-mouthed. They might only have met one another relatively recently, but he was still her cousin, Sadie reminded herself loyally. She might not approve of the things he did, or the way he lived his life, but she couldn't help but be emotionally affected by the way he had come to her support against Leon.

'Francine is virtually bankrupt—and so am I. Worse than that, I have commitments....'

'Commitments?' Sadie repeated uneasily.

'All right, if you will have it, debts,' Raoul admitted, flinging out one arm in a gesture of open despair. 'I have debts, Sadie. There! I have been forced to tell you what I had hoped not to have to do. I am in your hands now, Sadie, and if you don't help me by agreeing not just to this sale but to giving your expertise to Francine then I shall be facing financial ruin.'

Somewhere in the back of Sadie's mind a tiny warning bell rang. It was a small, sharp and instinctive feeling that Raoul was not being either totally honest or totally genuine. But loyally she refused to listen to it. Even so, a little hesitantly, she began, 'I...I...' and then stopped.

Raoul swung round and exclaimed joyously, 'You'll do it? Oh, Sadie, thank you. Thank you.' He was holding her in his arms. Hugging her, kissing her on both cheeks and then again as his pleasure and relief overwhelmed him. 'I cannot tell you what this means to me.'

There were actually tears in his eyes, as well as in his voice, Sadie recognised.

'You don't know what a weight off my shoulders it will be to get this contract signed...and to get away from here,' he added, giving the dusty room a dismissive, disparaging look.

'Get away?' Sadie queried.

'Yes. This place is obviously part of the deal, and quite frankly I am relieved that it is. I cannot wait to buy myself a decent modern apartment. But first I have to make a short trip...a family matter...an elderly relative on my mother's side. She lives outside Paris in...in straitened circumstances. She is my godmother, and I want to do a little something to help her. Your agreement to the sale of Francine means that I shall be able to do so!'

He cleared his throat and his voice thickened. 'I shall let Leon know what you have said. I can't tell you how much your agreement means to me, Sadie. With the money I receive from Leon I shall be able to see that Tante Amelie receives the care she needs. It is the least I can do. And you, Sadie—I expect you will be wanting to return to your own home. There will be much for you to do there, I know, before you begin working for Francine and Leon!'

Sadie frowned. She supposed she should not have been surprised to discover that her grandmother's childhood home was to be included in the sale of the business, but she owned that she was surprised by Raoul's revelations about his ailing godmother! And she would have to return to Pembroke, of course. But she had not planned to do so as yet.

'Won't Leon want to…to discuss his plans with me?' she questioned Raoul.

'Yes, indeed, but not right now. I suspect he will want to wait until after the formalities of the contract being signed for that.'

Disconcerted, Sadie digested her disappointment at the thought of not seeing Leon again for some time. She hadn't actually wanted to see him, had she? That wasn't why she was changing her mind,was it? Because…

No, of course it wasn't! How could it be? She barely knew the man!

Guessing from the way he kept looking at his watch that Raoul had other things to do, Sadie took her leave of him.

She might as well see out her stay in France, she decided, as she got into her car. And then if Leon did want to discuss anything with her over the next couple of days she would be on hand.

Her decision was based entirely on common sense, she assured herself as she pulled out into the traffic. Common sense. That was all…nothing else, she assured herself firmly.

Raoul waited until he was sure that Sadie had gone before telephoning Leon, his fingers drumming impatiently on the wall as he waited for Leon to answer his call. When he did, Raoul began immediately.

'I've spoken to Sadie, and it is just as I said it would be, Leon,' Raoul announced boastfully. 'I soon made her see reason. All you need to do now is get the contracts organised. Oh, by the way, speaking of the contracts—I was wondering…is there any way you could let me have an advance on the buyout figure? Only I've got a couple of obligations I'd like to get cleared up.'

Leon frowned as he listened to Raoul. He knew all about Raoul's debts, having had him thoroughly investigated prior to their negotiations. Illogically, he acknowledged that whilst he was relieved to hear that Raoul had managed to talk Sadie round, he also felt surprised, and almost a little bit disappointed that she had given in to her cousin so easily. Somehow he had expected her to put up more of a fight!

Suspiciously, he challenged Raoul.

'You haven't forgotten what I said to you about my not being agreeable to changing my decision on the ingredients of any new scent she creates, have you, Raoul?'

'Of course not,' Raoul responded promptly.

'Did she say why she had changed her mind?' Leon probed.

On the other end of the line Raoul frowned in irritation. Leon was asking for too many questions. Why on earth couldn't he simply accept what he was saying to him?

'She's a woman, Leon,' Raoul told him. 'Who knows why they do the things they do? About that advance... I need to leave Grasse for a few days, and...'

'I shall arrange for five hundred thousand euros to be transferred into your account today, Raoul.'

'Five hundred thousand—that is all?'

He could hear the disappointment in the other man's voice.

'Five hundred thousand,' Leon confirmed grimly. 'Take it or leave it!'

After Raoul had rung off, Leon stared frowningly through the open glass door of his suite. His attention was not focused on the stunning view that lay beyond his private balcony, but instead on something or rather someone that the male core of his memory found even more stunning.

Sadie!

It still surprised him that she had changed her mind and given in, agreeing not just to the sale of Francine to him but also agreed to work for him as well. Somehow it seemed a little out of character. Almost as if she'd submitted to him...

Hastily he dragged his thoughts back from the brink they were careering towards and reminded himself that he had work to do!

Since leaving Grasse earlier he had spent far more time than he wanted to admit thinking about her! And not just because of the problems she was causing him with the takeover. Not just? Be honest, he derided himself Not at all! No, the reason she had gained so much control inside

his head was quite simply because she, or rather his reaction to her, his awareness of her, his desire for her, had
assumed far too much control of his senses!

To put it bluntly, he ached for her in a way that had
not just caught him off guard, but was also actively making him…

Making him what? Making him want to rewind life
right back to that second when he had first seen her in
Cannes, so that he could do what every male instinct his
body was packed with had urged him to do then? Pick
her up in his arms, get her the hell out of there and take
her somewhere where….

It was at times like this that his Greek blood was most
at odds with his Australian upbringing, Leon acknowledged wryly. Right now, hormonally he was quite definitely all Greek male, but cerebrally—thank heaven—a
part of him remained an Aussie businessman! And that
was the part of him he needed most to focus on!

He had certainly enjoyed focusing on Sadie, he mused.
He had never liked over-thin women, and Sadie was just
right—her waist so tiny he could span it with his hands,
her hips sexily curved, her legs long…long enough to
wrap right around him when he…and her breasts. Ah,
her breasts… Just the thought of touching them, holding
them, brushing his lips against their tender quivering
crests and then…

Leon gave a low groan and closed his eyes. Bad mistake, since immediately a vision of Sadie formed behind
his shuttered eyelids. He must be going crazy—either that
or he was well on his way to falling head over heels in
love with her.

In love? In lust, more like! Anyway, falling in love
right now was a complication he definitely did not need

in his life. Unlike Sadie. He needed *her* all right. In his
life. In his arms. In his bed...

Raoul had told him that she was going back to England
and Leon told himself that he ought to be glad!

His grandmother would certainly have enjoyed seeing
him in the state of turmoil he was in right now!

Thinking of his grandmother made Leon frown again.
He had been just fourteen when she died. A sensitive age,
which was no doubt why—

His mobile phone rang, breaking his train of thought.

Was she doing the right thing? Sadie asked herself so-
berly as she parked her car in the hotel car park and made
her way to her room.

She wished passionately that her grandmother were
here for her to talk to. Would she approve of what she
was doing? The wave of euphoria which had carried her
back to Grasse had receded now, leaving her feeling
shaky and insecure. What if she couldn't create a saleable
perfume? And, even if she did, what made her think that
her scent could succeed where so many others had failed?
They lived in a different world now from the one in
which the classic scents had been created. Consumers
were more demanding, more fickle—but if she could succeed...if she could create a new scent that would take
the world by storm and...

She was beginning to feel light-headed with excitement again. What if, between them, she and Leon...?

Between them? She and Leon? A fresh surge of excitement gripped her, but this one had nothing whatsoever to do with the creation of a new scent!

Why didn't she give in and admit it to herself? She
had been attracted to Leon the first moment she had
seen him.

Attracted to him! To describe her feelings as mere attraction was like trying to compare cologne with full-strength perfume.

Her heart started to thud, her palms suddenly becoming damp. Why was it that the look in one particular man's eyes could make a woman feel so...? Hot-cheeked, Sadie acknowledged that she did not want to explore just what it was that Leon made her feel right now! At least not in public.

'I just hope that I'm doing the right thing.'

Sadie's voice wobbled a little, and she held her mobile just that little bit tighter as she voiced her uncertainty to her friend.

On the other end of the line Mary responded bracingly.

'Well, it certainly sounds to me as though you are. Sometimes you just have to follow your instincts and your heart, Sadie, no matter how risky it might seem.'

Her heart! That organ started to thump erratically at the thought that she had betrayed herself so easily to her friend. How could Mary have guessed from what she had told her about her emergent feelings for Leon? She had barely mentioned him!

'Your kind of work isn't merely a career choice, Sadie, it's a vocation, and when a person has your kind of talent—well, then they need to be able to fulfil the need it gives them and follow the direction of their heart, rather than make cerebral decisions!'

Her work! Mary was talking about her work, not about Leon!

'It is a once in a lifetime opportunity,' Sadie agreed excitedly. 'But—'

'No more buts,' Mary told her firmly. 'You go for it, girl!'

She had spent longer talking to her friend on the telephone than she had realised, Sadie recognised ten
minutes after she had ended the call, when the grumbling
protest of her stomach made her look at her watch. It was
almost eight o'clock and she hadn't eaten since breakfast!

Showering quickly, Sadie redressed in an elegant taupe
silk dress she had spotted in an expensive boutique's sale
in Paris, slipping her bare feet into a pair of kitten-heeled
sandals and gathering up a cream cashmere wrap just in
case the evening air proved chilly.

It was only a five-minute walk from the rooms to the
main hotel, and as Sadie picked her way along the prettily
illuminated path and down the several flights of stone
steps she paused to look out across the valley, to where
the lights of the town twinkled in the distance.

As she crossed the car park *en route* for the hotel foyer
she noticed that it was busy with cars, but thought no
more about it, smiling briefly at the receptionist as she
made her way across the tiled floor and then walked
down the stairs and through the lower level foyer into
the cocktail bar.

It had bemused her a little the first time she had walked
into this bar, to recognise that it was styled very much
in the manner of a gracious English country house—even
to the extent of having a log-burning fire—but this hotel
was not occupied merely in the summer, she acknowledged, but all the year round by those who wished to use
its spa facilities. The cocktail bar was certainly very comfortable and welcoming.

The lower foyer, through which she had just walked,
had elegant French windows which opened out onto a
large paved patio area where guests could sit at wrought-
iron tables and look out across the valley. Tonight the
patio was crowded with several large groups of diners,

Sadie noticed as she headed for the entrance to the dining room and the *maître d'*.

'A table for dinner? *Madame*, I am sorry but that is not possible. We are fully booked,' he told her when she asked for a table.

Sadie stared at him.

'But I am a hotel resident,' she protested. Delicious food smells from the meal being served to a table of diners just inside the doorway were informing her just how very hungry she really was. Her stomach was actually growling.

The *maître d'* looked sorrowful and spread his hands.

'I am so sorry, but I think you will have seen in your room that hotel guests are requested to make prior reservations for dinner. We are a Michelin-starred restaurant, and many people drive out from Cannes to eat here.'

Sadie's heart was sinking deeper with every word he said. It was true that there was a notice in her room warning guests about the limited availability of tables for dinner.

'There are several very good restaurants in the old town of Mougins,' the *maître d'* informed her helpfully. 'It is only a short walk from here, and a very pretty place. It gets many tourists.'

Sadie sighed. Whilst she didn't mind eating alone in a hotel restaurant, she was loath to do so further afield. She *had* planned to visit the old town of Mougins, but during the daytime.

Ruefully she acknowledged that she ought to have pre-booked her dinner reservation, and realized that she was now going to have to return to her room and order a meal there, from Room Service. She had just thanked the *maître d'* and was making her way through the now extremely busy bar, when she suddenly saw Leon on the other side of the room.

He was walking towards her and had obviously seen her. Immediately her face lit up, a giddy sensation, a heady mixture of thrilling excitement, shock, and pleasure, flooding her body with breathless delight.

'Leon!' she exclaimed as he came towards her. 'What are you doing here?'

His calm, 'Actually, I'm staying here,' took her thrilled delight down a few notches, and she had to control her expression to stop herself from betraying her disappointment. He had not come looking for her, as she had originally deliriously believed.

'And you?' he queried. 'Are you dining here?'

He looked and sounded so coolly remote that her heart banged uncomfortably against her chest wall whilst she battled against the feeling of disappointment that was filling her.

The reality of him was so different from the fantasies she had been building inside her head all afternoon. He looked so austere, so disapproving and remote, so very much the man she remembered from their first encounter—right down to the immaculate shirt and suit.

The happiness and expectation that had fuelled her day was leaking out of her, and she was miserably conscious of the way in which Leon was looking over her shoulder and beyond her, as though in search of someone! Another woman perhaps? Did he have a dinner date?

Lifting her chin she told him bravely, 'Actually, no, I'm not dining here this evening, Coincidentally, I am also staying here.' There was no way she wanted him thinking she had booked in because she knew he was staying at this hotel. After all; she hadn't realized that he was. 'But unfortunately—obviously unlike you—I neglected to make a reservation for dinner. The *maître d'* has suggested that I walk into the old town and—'

'What? On your own? You are doing no such thing.' Leon stopped her authoritatively 'I'm surprised that he suggested such a thing to a woman on her own. You *are* on your own, I take it?'

He wasn't looking over her shoulder any more. In fact he was looking right at her, and his eyes, like his voice, had warmed—as though…as though…

'Yes. Yes, I am…' Sadie agreed weakly. 'I… Whoops.' She gave a small gasp as a new crowd of people pressed into the confined space of the bar, one of whom inadvertently bumping into her and causing her to stagger slightly.

Immediately Leon reached out for her, drawing her towards him. So close to him, in fact, that all it would have taken for their bodies to actually touch would be for her to take one good deep breath. And, even though she was in no real danger of being pushed or crushed by the crowd, his arm was still curled protectively around her.

'Look, it's getting like a beer garden in here,' he told her. 'Since I've got a table booked, why don't you join me?'

'Oh, no!' Sadie protested immediately. 'I didn't tell you because—'

'I did!' Leon told her softly.

The cold ice she had previously seen in his eyes had melted and turned into… Dizzily, she acknowledged that she could not find the right words to describe the incredible heat and sensuality that was burning in the green gaze he'd turned on her. All she could think of was what it was doing to her…

'Do you think that's a good idea?' Sadie couldn't help protesting.

'Why shouldn't it be?' Leon retaliated.

Sadie could think of a hundred reasons, all of which had to do with the fact that she was already dangerously aware of him and potentially responsive to him, without doing something that was bound to encourage her vulnerable emotions to start rioting totally out of control!

'Well, in view of the professional situation between us…' she began a little lamely, not wanting to admit to him the real reason why she felt that having dinner with him might not be a good idea.

But Leon wouldn't allow her to continue, saying immediately, 'Why don't we draw a line under all of that and start again? Call a truce? I've spoken to Raoul…'

Even though she knew she was being idiotic, Sadie couldn't quite suppress her small spurt of disappointment when she realised that Leon was talking to her as a business colleague, not as a woman he wanted to get to know personally.

'Oh, have you?' she answered him.

'I have,' he confirmed, 'and I can't tell you how pleased I am to hear about your decision, Sadie.'

'It seemed the best thing to do.' Sadie paused, wanting to tell him how pleased she was that he had backed down over the use of natural raw materials. But before she could continue Leon shook his head.

'Part of the truce is no business talk tonight.'

'You never said that before.'

'Didn't I?' The corners of his eyes crinkled with amusement. He really was heart-stoppingly sexy, Sadie acknowledged giddily. 'Ah, well, I'm saying it now!'

'But if we don't talk about business, then what—?'

Sadie stopped and blushed as she saw the way he was looking at her.

'Oh, I think we'll find that we have plenty of things to say to one another,' Leon told her softly.

Sadie didn't make any reply. She was far too conscious of the fact that she was dangerously close to wanting much more from him than a simple business relationship!

He was looking away from her and in the direction of the *maître d'* who was hurrying over. Turning towards him, Leon said something quietly and the other man ushered them both to Leon's table.

Sadie could see the subtle feminine interested looks Leon was attracting from the women diners at the other tables as they were led to their own. Predictably, he had been given a table in a prime position, and as the waiter pulled out a chair for her Sadie couldn't help feeling glad that she had chosen to wear her silk dress. It might not be as dramatic as some of the outfits several of the other women were wearing, but thanks to her grandmother she knew how to choose clothes that suited her.

Sadie had barely opened her menu when another waiter arrived, carrying a bottle of champagne and two glasses.

Wide-eyed, she looked at Leon.

'I hope you don't mind,' he told her softly. 'Only it seemed appropriate. To celebrate.'

Sadie couldn't drag her gaze away from his. Why on earth had she ever thought his eyes cold? They were anything but. And as for his smile... A funny aching sensation had begun to spread from the direction of her heart all the way down through her body right into her toes, making her curl them protectively inside her sandals!

'Well, yes...' she agreed, trying to sound nonchalant and sophisticated. 'Only Raoul did say it could be a few days before the contracts were ready for us all to sign, and since he isn't here...'

The smile curling Leon's mouth deepened and his eyes started to crinkle at the corners.

'It wasn't the prospect of us signing the contracts I wanted to celebrate,' he told her in a voice that sounded like dark melting chocolate.

'It...it wasn't...?' Agitatedly, Sadie picked up her glass of champagne.

'No, it wasn't,' Leon agreed, watching her with a gaze so sensual and exciting that Sadie just knew her whole body was about to start quivering with delight in response to it.

'Aren't you going to ask me what I *am* celebrating?' he prompted huskily.

'I...er...' Sadie took a deep gulp of her champagne and then gasped as the bubbles hit the back of her throat and exploded. She coughed and put her glass down.

'I'm sorry,' she apologised, her face burning at her own lack of sophistication.

'What's wrong? Don't you like champagne?' Leon teased her.

'Well, I do,' Sadie told him. 'Only I'm not much of a drinker, really. I suppose it comes of having been brought up by my grandmother... She was a bit old-fashioned about such things by modern standards.'

'Why did your grandmother bring you up?'

He was frowning now, but not in a disapproving or condemnatory way, Sadie noticed. No, he was looking at her as though he was genuinely interested in discovering more about her! A sweetly sharp thrill of excitement spun through her.

'My mother died shortly after I was born, and Dad— well, he had to work. So Grandmère brought me up, and then Dad remarried.' She paused awkwardly, not wanting him to think she was trying to make him feel sympathetic towards her. 'Well, Melanie—my stepmother—she was younger than Dad, and I don't think she was too keen on the idea of taking on a soon-to-be teenage stepdaughter. Anyway, I was happy to stay with Grandmère.'

'I see…'

He was looking at her in the most direct and yet somehow very tender way, Sadie recognised. A way that made her feel as though she could almost tell him just how hurt she had felt, knowing that her stepmother didn't want her and that her father did not love her enough to insist that she was allowed to be a part of their lives.

'I too had a very close relationship with my grandmother,' Leon told her quietly.

For a moment they looked at one another in silence. They were, Sadie recognised, two people suddenly discovering that they had more in common than they had realised.

'Your grandmother was Greek, wasn't she?' Sadie asked hesitantly, not wanting to pry and yet suddenly desperate to learn as much about him as she could, for him to be the one to tell her!

'Yes. Like you, with your grandmother, I was very close to her. My parents both worked in the business my father was building, and my grandmother lived with us and looked after me. She died when I was fourteen.' His frown deepened. 'It was a very bad time for the family.'

'You still miss her?' Sadie guessed.

'Yes,' he agreed gruffly. 'She didn't have the easiest of lives—' His mouth twisted a little bitterly. 'And that is an understatement. She had an extremely hard life. Her parents emigrated to Australia to escape from poverty at home. Her mother died before they reached Sydney and her father was so grief stricken that he began to drink. My grandmother brought up her brothers and sisters virtually single-handed, and looked after her father as well, when she was little more than a child herself! She was just twelve when they arrived in Australia, and twenty-four when she married my grandfather. She was working as a ladies' maid when he met her, and in those days anyone in service was not allowed to get married. She wouldn't leave her job because she still had her father to support.'

'She must have been a wonderful person,' Sadie told him softly.

'She was,' he agreed.

There was a look in his eyes she couldn't analyse, Sadie acknowledged. A look which held bitterness and anger. A look which for some reason right now he seemed to be directing right at her!

'You're wearing your perfume,' he said abruptly changing the subject

Sadie nodded her head, trying not to betray the fact she was pleased he had noticed.

'Is it very different from the original Myrrh?'

'A little,' she told him, the realisation that his interest had been of a business rather than a personal nature turning her pleasure to disappointment. Rather briskly, she added, 'The original perfume, like most perfumes of its time, was much stronger than women want to wear to-day—and, of course, very expensive.'

'Expensive and exclusive,' Leon agreed curtly. 'In fact, a luxury that most ordinary women could never hope to enjoy!'

To Sadie's bewilderment his expression as well as his voice once again suddenly changed, becoming closed and forbidding.

'Have you decided want you want to eat yet?' he asked grimly.

Sadie looked at him, tempted to ask what it was she had said that had caused him to withdraw so sharply from her, but instead she simply told him very coolly and distantly that, yes, she was ready to order.

'How old were you when you first knew that you had a ''nose''?'

Their first course had just arrived, and Sadie looked across at Leon a little warily. But whatever it was that had caused that momentary harsh bleakness to harden his expression had gone, and he was once more smiling warmly at her.

'I don't know,' she admitted. 'I just sort of grew up knowing that I wanted to create perfume. My grandmother encouraged me, of course. She was born at the wrong time, I think, looking back now. She would have loved to have taken over the business, but as a girl with a brother that was just not an option.'

'I have gathered that there was some discord between them,' Leon acknowledged, and he looked encouragingly at her, obviously wanting to learn more.

'My great-uncle was a gambler, and he ran down the business to finance his gambling habit. My grandmother hated what he did, and I think she ended up hating him too,' Sadie admitted. 'A rift developed between them which was exacerbated by the fact that my grandmother had married an Englishman and lived so far away from him. Still, she felt so passionately about the business...'

'A passion which she obviously passed on to you,' Leon interrupted her.

Sadie smiled.

'My grandmother was a very passionate person.'

'And so, I imagine, are you. Very passionate!'

Across the table their glances met and locked. Sadie discovered she was only able to breathe shallowly, her heart bouncing frantically around her chest, making her feel as though she wanted to press her hands to her body to keep it still.

The silence between them, the intimacy of their locked gazes, was the most exciting sensation she had ever experienced, she acknowledged dizzily. Her food was completely forgotten—Leon was her food, her need, her every sustenance both physical and emotional. If he were to reach out now, take hold of her hand and lead her from the table, she knew beyond any doubt that she would go with him.

'You can't possibly know that. I...' Her voice was a papery dry whisper, a muted husk of sound, her eyes huge, her pupils dilated.

'I do know it.' Leon stopped her. His own voice was tense, low and raw with an open hunger that made Sadie shudder violently.

'I know exactly how you will feel in my arms, Sadie, how you will taste, how passionately you will respond to me in my bed.'

What the hell was he doing? Leon wondered savagely as he heard what he was saying almost as though he was standing outside himself and listening. From the moment he had taken over the family business on his twenty-first birthday, Leon had dedicated himself totally to its success. Nothing and no one had ever threatened to come between him and that dedication—until now!

For the first time in his life Leon could feel himself being pulled in different directions emotionally. Had he gone completely mad? Totally lost the plot? Okay, so

Sadie was one delectably desirable woman. But that didn't mean...

The way she was looking at him made his body clench, and a surge of desire as fierce as the kick of a mule powered through his belly.

This wasn't something he had written down in his mental checklist of life goals. Not now and quite definitely not ever with *this* particular woman!

So why wasn't he doing something about it? Why wasn't he getting a grip and forcing his unwanted desire for her to shrivel into nothing? Because he didn't want to or because he couldn't do so? Because he was already in way way over his head and not even thinking about trying to save himself?

A small shudder ripped through Sadie, openly visible to him, and his own body reacted. Responded! Hell, but no woman had affected him like this in public since he had left his teenage days behind him. It was a damn good job that the table covered the visible evidence of his arousal.

He moved a little uncomfortably in his seat, cursing softly to himself.

Sadie held her breath as she saw the way Leon's eyes burned with sexual awareness as he monitored her reaction.

She could hardly breathe normally, never mind think of eating! Frantically she tried to come up with something banal to say, to extinguish the almost palpable aura of sexual heat surrounding them. But her brain was simply refusing to co-operate. If she didn't manage to break the sensual intensity of the gaze they were sharing Sadie didn't know what might happen! Or, rather, she knew perfectly well what her body was hoping would happen!

And that knowledge was making her feel both more excited than she had ever felt in her whole life and more apprehensive as well!

Someone at a nearby table pushed back their chair, and the scraping noise caused Leon to look in that direction. Dizzily Sadie dragged great gulps of air into her lungs and picked up her fork.

CHAPTER FOUR

SINCE Leon had already determined to put things between them back on a sensible, businesslike footing at the very first chance he got, why, when Sadie had taken the opportunity to do exactly that, was he reacting as though she was somehow challenging him? And why was he actively looking for ways to break through the social barriers she had thrown up and return things to a much more personal level? Leon asked himself derisively.

He had never thought of himself as the kind of man so needy, and lacking in self-esteem as to have to verbally force a woman to be aware of him sexually, but right now...

He looked at Sadie's mouth. It was soft and full, and if she was wearing any lipstick it was so natural as to be virtually indiscernible. He hated kissing women who caked their mouths in red grease! Kissing Sadie's mouth, in fact kissing any bit of Sadie, would be a pleasure he would give his eye teeth for right now!

Desperate to bring her rioting emotions and desires under control, Sadie waited until their main course had been served before clearing her throat and asking politely, 'What made you decide to buy Francine?'

For a moment she thought that he wasn't going to reply, but then he looked at her and her heart did a foolish somersault.

'It just seemed a natural progression. We are a luxury goods group, after all.' Right now he didn't want to discuss his business affairs with Sadie. In fact he didn't really want to talk about anything with her at all. At the moment the kind of communication he wanted to share with Sadie involved using their lips for something much more intimate than phrasing words!

Although Leon had spoken naturally enough in answer to her question, Sadie had felt as though he was measuring his words, as if somehow he was having to guard what he said, she reflected. But she was guiltily aware that, although she had been listening to his words, a wickedly wanton streak in herself she had not realised she possessed had been focusing on Leon's mouth in an altogether far too intimate way!

'We made a deal that we weren't going to talk about business,' Leon reminded her.

Sadie's heart banged so loudly against her ribs that she was too worried that he might have heard it to think about anything else.

'This steak is the best I've tasted in a long time,' Leon told Sadie enthusiastically.

He had been caught slightly on the hop by Sadie's unexpected question about his reasons for acquiring Francine. Wanting her was one thing. Discussing his grandmother with her was another! He knew that it was his own pride that made him feel so immediately protective of his grandmother, so unwilling to discuss the real reason why he so much wanted to acquire Francine and Myrrh.

The truth was that he had never forgotten how he had felt as a youngster, when his grandmother had told him the story of how when she had been a ladies' maid she had yearned to be able to wear the exotic and expensive perfume worn by her mistress.

'It was called Myrrh,' his grandmother had told him with a sigh, 'and it was the most beautiful perfume ever.'

'Couldn't you have bought some?' his younger self had asked her naïvely.

She had smiled sadly and shaken her head, ruffling his hair with a hand gnarled and deformed by years of hard domestic work.

'Leon, just one small bottle would have cost more than I would have earned in five years,' she had told him. 'Perfume like that wasn't created for women like me!'

As he had seen the look in her eyes Leon had sworn there and then that one day his grandmother would own a bottle of the best and the most expensive perfume in the world, and that he would buy it for her. Only she had died before he had been able to make good that promise. But he had never forgotten that he had made it, and never ceased regretting that he hadn't been able to keep it. And he had certainly never forgotten *why* he had made it, which was why he'd felt so antagonistic towards Sadie's original refusal to create a new perfume that would be inexpensive enough for every woman to wear and enjoy.

But fortunately Sadie had seen sense, and at last the Myrrh scent was going to belong to him! It was too late for his grandmother to enjoy, but at least he would have the satisfaction of knowing that the grandson of the woman who hadn't been able to afford to buy the smallest bottle of the scent now owned the whole company! And if it was the last thing he did he intended to make sure that every woman who wanted to would be able to afford to wear a Francine perfume!

And so he had deliberately not told his board the reasons for his determination to acquire Francine. There was no way he was going to make himself vulnerable to anyone by admitting that he had been motivated to buy Francine out of sentiment. He would never hand out that kind of information and give others the opportunity to crucify him! As they undoubtedly would. The business world he operated in traded in financial gains, not emotional ones. And it only respected the men who made those financial gains.

Leon had grown up in a tough world, watching his parents struggling to establish the business—and then, just when the business had been on the verge of becoming very profitable, he'd seen them very nearly lose it. The shock and stress of that event had undermined his father's health and left him permanently weakened physically. Witnessing such traumatic events had given Leon a fierce, youthful resolve to do all he could to protect his family, to make the business so financially stable and secure that he would never again have to see his father's face grey with defeat and despair, or his mother's eyes shining with frightened tears.

He might have taken his parents' business and built it into the successful and profitable empire it was today, he might be a billionaire whose wealth could open any door for him, but deep down inside there was a part of him that still felt the anguish and the anger he had experienced as a fourteen-year-old, witnessing his parents' fear, just as he still remembered listening to his grandmother describe how her poverty had sometimes humiliated her.

His children would be told all about their great-grandmother, and they would be brought up to respect and revere her memory, to understand that money could not buy spirit or character or love. If Sadie objected to that then she was not the woman he believed her to be...

Leon put down his cutlery with a clatter that made Sadie stare at him in confusion and wonder just what had caused that look of arrested shock she could see in his eyes. But before she could question him, however, he had distracted her by asking if she had as yet tried any of the hotel's spa facilities.

'No I haven't,' she admitted. 'Have you?'

'No,' Leon acknowledged. 'There hasn't really been time.'

Sadie gave a small but very luxurious sigh. It was over an hour since they had finished their meal and come into the bar, where Leon had escorted her over to one of the seductively comfortable squashy sofas before going to order their drinks.

They were the only people left there, apart from the bar staff, and the logs on the fire had burned down to glowing ashes. She couldn't say just what she and Leon had talked about—the time had flown by on wings of exultation and delight. It was almost as though Leon could actually sense what she was thinking—so much so that every time she had been tempted to forget their pact and talk to him about her excited plans for the future, and the new perfume she hoped to create, he'd somehow stopped her, sidelining their conversation into another direction. And all the time…all the time…every minute, every second, he had been looking at her in such a way that…

'It looks like we've outstayed our welcome,' Leon told her now, with an amused look at the barman, very purposefully cleaning up. 'I'll walk you back to your room,' he added as Sadie stood up.

Outside it was cool enough for her to be glad she had brought her wrap—and she was even more pleased when without a word Leon took it from her and draped it gently over her shoulders. Was it her imagination or did his fingers really stroke slowly against her bare skin before he stepped back from her?

The path which wound up along the hillside and through the gardens was well illuminated by the strategically placed lighting. The sky was a blue-black dome of velvet, sprinkled with diamond-bright stars, with the thin sliver of a crescent moon.

The path curved and slipped between a small stand of trees into a hidden grove of scented darkness, which took Sadie by surprise, causing her to half stumble on an unseen step.

Immediately Leon reached out to steady her.

'Thanks.' Although the ground was in darkness there was enough light from the moon for her to see his features. The intensity of his gaze her made her heart thump frantically. 'I didn't realise there was a step there.' It was disconcerting to know how at odds with the way she was feeling the bland mundanity of her words was.

'No. I'm surprised the hotel management hasn't had this area better lit. Surprised, but extremely pleased,' Leon told her rawly.

'Pleased?' Was he actually saying what she thought he was saying? Sadie's heart was doing more than merely thumping now; it was practically turning excited cartwheels! Instinctively she looked up at Leon, and the hungry look in his eyes caused the whole world to spin dizzily round her. She stood very still.

Slowly Leon lowered his head, his mouth seeking her own. Silently she waited, hardly daring to breathe in case she broke the spell that was binding them together in the magical and intimate darkness.

His lips touched hers, firm, warm, sure and knowledgeable, making her feel...

Making her feel like a woman, Sadie acknowledged giddily. Like a very desirable woman.

Strong male hands drew her closer, one resting in the

small of her back, the other lifting to her neck, sliding beneath her hair, supporting her head as the pressure of his kiss tipped it backwards.

Sadie exhaled a disbelieving shaky whisper of breath before eagerly parting her lips to the probing thrust of Leon's tongue. She could feel the solid trunk of a tree behind her shoulders, and yet had no memory of having stepped backwards. Leon's hand had left the small of her back and travelled to the rounded curve of her bottom, urging her into his own body.

With a fierce thrill of delight she recognised his arousal, her body reacting to it with a sensual abandon that had her pushing her hips against him, revelling in the immediate and passionate response of his hands and his mouth as he gripped her harder and thrust his tongue deeper into the eager softness of her mouth.

Her own arms were wrapped tightly around him now, her breasts sensitised by the movement of her body against his. In her mind she could already picture his hands covering their nakedness, feel the fierce tug of his mouth against her nipples.

She shuddered violently at her own thoughts. A sharp spike of shock pierced through her, only to be overwhelmed by a fresh wave of aching longing as Leon pressed her even more closely to his body.

He felt excitingly hard and... Instinctively Sadie's mind shied away from what she was thinking, imagining...

She wasn't in the habit of assessing a man's virility in terms of shape and size, and she most certainly wasn't in the habit of getting excited about them—or him!

What had happened to her normal reserve? Not to mention the moral objections...the sheer common sense she should be heeding?

Leon's mouth was moving along her jaw and towards her ear, leaving a trail of delicate kisses that filled her with stunning delight. Dizzily Sadie acknowledged that just the whisper of his breath…his lips against her skin…was sending her crazy. Not that he was exactly immune to the reaction he was arousing in her, judging by the way he was gripping her hips and pulling her tightly against his body, Sadie realised with a fierce thrill of female pleasure.

'The way you're making me feel I could take you here and now, do you know that?' Leon groaned against her ear, confirming her thoughts and sending her pulse rocketing out of control whilst the images inside her head became even more explicit and steamy.

Again she wondered—where was her normal, sane and sensible self that should have been objecting sharply and immediately to what he was saying? Why was she moving her body even closer to his instead of pulling herself away?

Sadie didn't know, and what was more she didn't care. In fact, if Leon chose to put his threat into action, she didn't think she would be able to object. Object…? She was aching so badly for him that…

Now it was her turn to moan out loud with delight as his hand moved up her body and cupped her breast. Just the feel of his thumb-tip rubbing sensuously across her tight, aching nipple made her bite on her bottom lip to stop herself from begging him to take off her top and expose her breast to his gaze, his touch and the hot, hard caress of his mouth.

Frantically she tensed her muscles, squeezing her thighs together as she felt the surge of longing rocket through her.

As though he guessed what was happening to her,

Leon cupped her hip, his fingers kneading her rhythmically.

She was leaning fully against the tree now, letting it take the weight of her body whilst Leon's hands sensitively explored every inch of her, making her quiver from head to foot in open longing.

When his hand stroked gently between her legs she groaned huskily and shuddered.

'Sadie…' As Leon took her hand and placed it against his own body she almost sobbed with pleasure. Her hands were long and slender, but the hard swollen length of him extended beyond her outstretched fingertips. Sadie closed her eyes, pleasure a dark velvet blanket of sensuality behind her eyelids. She ached as though she had a fever for the feel of him inside her. She'd had no idea there could be desire like this—instant, immediate, hot and hungry, a need that burned everything else into oblivion and drove a person relentlessly until it was sated.

No doubt in Leon's eyes, she decided helplessly, she was totally unworldly and naïve not to have experienced something like this before. Unlike him!

How many times…how many women…? That thought burned through her in a hot agony of molten jealousy that stiffened her whole body.

'Sadie?'

Suddenly they both heard voices somewhere lower down the path. Immediately Leon released her and bent to pick up the shawl which had fallen from her shoulders.

Tucking her hand through his arm, he guided her back to the path. She was shaking so much she suspected she would have stumbled if he hadn't been holding on to her.

Unable to keep her feelings to herself, she burst out emotionally, 'I don't believe this is happening.'

'You don't believe or you don't want to believe it?' Leon challenged her.

Tiny tremors of reaction were still seizing her body, and Sadie knew that Leon must be aware of them. What an idiot he must think her, to get in such a state over a mere kiss. Only for her it hadn't been just a kiss, had it? For her...

'It's all right, Sadie,' she heard him telling her gently, when she was unable to answer his question. 'Will it help if I admit that I've been caught as much off guard by what happened back there as you? I can't pretend that I haven't spent all evening imagining what it would be like to take you to bed, but...'

'I...I don't do things like this,' Sadie told him stiffly, suddenly feeling exposed and vulnerable. 'I don't make a habit of...of this sort of thing. You might...'

'I might what?' he asked, disconcerting her when he guessed accurately. 'Were you thinking that I might go to bed with a different woman every night of the week? Is that what you're trying to say?'

Embarrassed, Sadie shook her head.

'I don't have any right to...to pry into your private life,' she told him awkwardly. 'It's just that I don't want you to think that I...'

'I haven't been to bed with a woman in over five years,' Leon told her curtly. 'I don't happen to approve of anyone sleeping around just for the hell of it. It's cheap and it's a health hazard. What happened tonight was—'

'You don't have to explain. I understand!' Sadie rushed in quickly. He was going to tell her that it had been a mistake, that things had got out of hand.

'You do? I wish to hell that I could say that,' Leon came back at her with harsh grimness. 'Right now—' he stopped and shook his head whilst Sadie held her breath, aching to have him complete what he had been going to say, and at the same time a little fearful in case he did!

They had almost reached the door to her room.

'Do you have any plans for tomorrow?' Leon asked her abruptly as he stood in front of her.

They were almost as close as they had been earlier, when he had kissed her. If she were to just shift her weight from one foot to the other she would be even closer!

Sadie looked at him. Her body was already overruling the cautious anxieties of her heart and the stern warnings of her head, telling her very forcibly that the only plans it wanted to have, included Leon and preferably complete privacy!

'Well, no...not really.' As her heart jumped and thumped around her ribcage, with an adrenalin-fuelled cocktail of complex emotions, Sadie berated herself inwardly. Why on earth hadn't she told him she was already busy, as she would normally have done? What was happening to her? Never in her life had she chosen danger over safety. It just wasn't her style!

Maybe it hadn't been, a little voice inside her head mocked her, but that had been before she'd met Leon!

'I'm driving out to see a *mas* I'm renting for the summer tomorrow. Why don't you come with me?'

'You're spending the whole summer here?' Sadie commented, unable to conceal her envy at the thought of being able to spend weeks on end enjoying the sunshine in a *mas*, as Provençal farmhouses were called.

Yes...I have a variety of business interests on the continent, and the farmhouse I am planning to rent would make an excellent base for me to work from.'

They were outside her door now, and the light on the

wall illuminated Sadie's expression as she looked up at him.

'A farmhouse?' she questioned, a little uncertainly.

'You don't sound very enthusiastic,' Leon commented wryly. 'What's wrong? Don't you like the countryside?' he asked her.

Immediately Sadie shook her head.

'No, I love it,' she told him vehemently.

'So?' The querying rise of Leon's eyebrows warned her that he intended to get an answer.

'Well, it's just that… Well, I just didn't think that you would be a country person. One always assumes, some-how, that a businessman will be city-based.' Sadie began, and then stopped, biting her lip.

But to her relief Leon didn't take offence at her com-ment, simply shrugging his shoulders and telling her eas-ily, 'I do have an apartment in Sydney, it's true. It's convenient for business, but given the choice I'd much rather spend my time at the winery my parents own, way out in the country. They're retired now, or supposed to be, but Dad's already talking about putting new vines in and upgrading their wine, despite the fact that he's got a bad heart and ought to be taking things easy!' He stopped and apologised. 'Sorry, you don't want to hear about my family.'

Sadie flicked her tongue-tip over her lips, aching to admit that there was nothing she wanted to learn about more—unless it was every tiny detail about Leon himself. What made him laugh, what kind of food he liked, which side of the bed he liked to sleep on…where he most liked to be touched and kissed…where…

'Well?' she heard him demanding softly.

Her face flared hot pink as for an instant she thought he had somehow read her mind, but then she realised he was waiting for her to respond to his invitation. She ought to turn it down, her own sense of self-preservation told her that, but instead of doing so she heard herself saying huskily, 'Thank you, yes. I...I'd love to join you.' To join him. To join *with* him...to...!

'Good!'

The look he gave her sent a thrill of dangerous pleasure zinging right through her. Helplessly she clenched her muscles against it, against the betraying sexual shudder she could feel gripping her.

Leon was smiling at her, his mouth curling up at the corners in the way that made her long to throw her arms around him and kiss every delicious centimetre of those tempting warm male lips. Especially where they curled so fascinatingly into the smile that made her heart somersault and sent a dizzying rush of pleasure showering through her.

Hastily Sadie averted her gaze from his mouth and tried instead to focus on a point somewhere beyond his left shoulder. But she was still excruciatingly conscious of him, and of her own longing for him. Where had it come from, this savage, clawing, aching, longing that had hit her out of nowhere, left her drugged, doped, dependent on the proximity of him?

When she had contemplated the prospect of falling in love in the past her mental meanderings had never come anywhere near encompassing anything like this! And they had certainly never allowed her to imagine anyone like Leon!

'Hell, Sadie, will you please stop looking at me like that?' Leon demanded savagely. 'Because if you don't I'm going to have to kiss you, and I warn you that if I do I'm not going to want to stop at just kissing you...' he continued fiercely.

Her face bright red, Sadie asked him quickly, 'I...what time shall I meet you in the morning?' She held her breath, not sure if she wanted Leon to stop speaking so erotically to her or not.

'Well, from my point of view it will probably facilitate matters if we have breakfast together,' Leon began.

'Together?' Sadie could hear the squeak of panic in her voice.

'I meant in the dining room, of course,' Leon assured her blandly. 'Unless...'

'Oh, the dining room. Yes, of course. Yes...er...what time? I...'

Listening to herself gabbling, Sadie wondered if Leon knew just how much she was longing to have the courage to simply reach out and wrap her arms around him, to stand on tiptoe and press her body the entire length of his whilst she kissed him in a way that would leave him in no doubt whatsoever about where she most wanted to have breakfast with him tomorrow morning!

Before he could guess what she was thinking she opened her handbag and searched for her key.

Ten minutes later, safely inside her room on her own, with the door locked, she told herself that it was relief she was feeling that Leon hadn't pushed or pressed to be allowed to come in with her—and not disappointment.

Still, she would be seeing him in the morning. Blissfully she hugged that thought to her, lost in a dreamy fantasy of sensual blue skies and an even more sensual man.

CHAPTER FIVE

'THAT'S what I like to see—a woman who enjoys her food.'

Sadie's toes curled into her shoes as Leon's warmly approving gaze embraced her.

He had telephoned her at seven o'clock, the ringing bringing her out of the shower, to ask her if she was awake and suggest that they meet up in the restaurant at eight.

'Awake—of course I'm awake,' she had responded indignantly, adding without thinking, 'I was actually in the shower.'

There was a small silence, and then Leon's voice, like warm honey melting down the telephone line, as he'd said thickly, 'I wish you hadn't told me that, Sadie!'

He hadn't said anything else, but Sadie had known immediately that he was picturing her naked—and what was more she had been doing some pretty sensual visualisation of the two of them together herself!

Just the thought of Leon naked in the shower with her was enough to make her skin prickle in sensual hunger.

She had dressed at top speed, donning a clean white tee shirt and a pair of beige linen cut-offs, and some white and beige trainers for comfort. A beige raffia bag embroidered with white daisies and her sunglasses had completed her preparations.

Leon had been waiting for her in the foyer of the hotel. Like her, he was casually dressed, his tee shirt revealing warmly tanned and strongly muscled arms.

'Good.' He smiled approvingly at her. 'I'm glad you've dressed casually. The *mas* is in a fairly remote place, and although it has its own swimming pool, and overlooks the sea itself, I've picked it because of its country location.'

Now, as she finished her fruit and reached for the delicious croissant she had selected from the lavish buffet table, Sadie turned to Leon and mentioned hesitantly, 'Raoul told me that your company will be acquiring the house in Grasse as well as the business attached to it.'

She couldn't help thinking how much this would have upset her grandmother. She had often told Sadie whilst she was growing up how much she missed her childhood home. Sadie had been too young then to suggest that her grandmother lower her pride and make contact with her brother, with a view to visiting Grasse and the house.

'You should see it, Sadie,' she had told her vehemently. 'It is as much a part of your heritage as your "nose".' When your grandfather saved me from the Germans and brought me to England I had no idea that I would never return to Grasse. My father would have been so angry and hurt if he had known what my brother did.'

Sadie had tried to find words to comfort her, but she had seen how much her grandmother had missed her home.

'Yes, that is part of the deal,' Leon agreed, picking up the coffee pot and refilling her empty cup for her.

'What will you do with it? Will you keep it or sell it?' Sadie asked him, wondering what it was about seeing such a strong sexy man performing this small domestic chore that made her insides melt.

'I don't know yet, and anyway the decision won't be

entirely mine to make. Why?' Leon questioned, giving her a keen look.

'No reason,' Sadie answered him hesitantly. Despite the physical intimacy they had shared she didn't feel mentally close enough to him to talk more about her grandmother.

Her reticence owed more to her own loyalty to her grandmother than a reluctance to confide in Leon. She was well aware that an outsider who had not known her grandmother might question her stubbornness in refusing to have anything to do with her estranged brother. And, for reasons she was not prepared to delve deeply into, it was becoming increasingly important to Sadie that Leon felt warmly and sympathetically towards the grandmother she had loved so much. After all, how could she give her love completely to a man who did not understand and accept Grandmère's little foibles?

Leon was still looking at her, with one dark eyebrow raised and an expression in his eyes that told her he knew she was being evasive.

Ruefully, she gave a small shrug.

'It's just that—well, there is so much family history attached to the house. I just think it would be very sad if it were to be sold off, or converted into offices or apartments like so many of the older buildings have been. If you were going to…to dispose of it…'

'You'd want first chance to buy it?' Leon guessed, wondering why, if she did want the property, she had not asked for it to be included in the package he was having put together for her in part exchange for the very generous lump sum she would be receiving for her share of the business.

Immediately Sadie shook her head.

'I'd love to,' she admitted, wrinkling her nose a little

as she added, 'But there's no way I could afford it. Even in its run-down state it would still be expensive, and I just don't have that kind of money. Not even if I sold my home in England.'

Leon frowned as he listened to her. Raoul had implied to him that Sadie came from a wealthy background— 'pampered and spoiled' had been just two of the words he had used to describe her. Even if Raoul had been lying, the sum he had agreed to pay him for the business and the property was, in his opinion, on the dangerous side of generous—and he knew that his board would agree with him.

Sadie would by virtue of her one-third holding in Francine receive one-third of that money. When he included in that sum the extra amount he had now offered, via Raoul, to pay in respect of Sadie giving up her own business to join the company, he was looking at a very large amount indeed—and Sadie's share was well in excess of what he knew to be the value of the Grasse property.

It was on the tip of his tongue to challenge her statement, and a small frown wrinkled his forehead as he contemplated what might lie behind Sadie's seemingly artless comment.

Could she actually be angling for him to offer to hand over the Grasse property to her? Somehow he hadn't thought of her as a person who was either manipulative or grasping—unlike her cousin. But he was enough of a businessman to respect the fact that she was in a position where, if she chose to do so, she could set an extremely high value on her expertise.

Unusually for Raoul, he had been unexpectedly and unhelpfully vague about what he thought Sadie's financial requirements might be for joining Francine, and so

Leon had sought the advice of a local firm of head-hunters, asking them what the going rate for a person of Sadie's skills would be. Once they had told him he had decided that in view of the fact she was giving up her stance on natural raw materials, and agreeing to create a new perfume, he had added a large extra amount onto the sum he had informed his legal team he would be paying her as a salary.

If she was after the Grasse house as an additional 'sweetener', though, she was going to be disappointed!

Aware of his unexpected and certainly unwanted with-drawal from her, but totally unaware of what Leon was thinking, Sadie questioned lightly, 'Is something wrong?'

'No, nothing at all,' Leon assured her smoothly. 'If you're ready, we ought to make a start. The *mas* is a good three hours' drive away.'

Relieved to see the sombre look replaced by a much warmer one, Sadie nodded her head.

The tables on the open air terrace of the restaurant where they had eaten their breakfast were filling up with other guests now, and Sadie was glad that they'd eaten early enough to have virtually had the place to them-selves.

This hotel would make a wonderful venue for honey-moons, she acknowledged as she stood up and Leon came to pull her chair back for her. What with its spa facilities and suites with their own private hot tubs. If she and Leon were sharing such a suite…

As he saw her eyes darken and her face flush, Leon wondered what it was that had brought that soft look to Sadie's eyes and caused her sudden intake of breath.

Standing close to her now, breathing in the warm scent of her, he wondered if he was being entirely wise in choosing to spend a whole day with her—especially after last night! And it wasn't the fiercely passionate kiss they had exchanged before going their separate ways he was thinking about, but the hours afterwards, when he had lain awake in bed, aching for her so much that he'd had to grit his teeth against the sheer intensity of it, and will the hard, angry throb of his erection to subside.

When Leon picked up the keys for the hire car he had ordered from the foyer, the receptionist announced, 'The hire car firm has asked me to apologise to you because unfortunately they have not been able to supply you with the car you requested. They have instead delivered a smaller one. Apparently there was a mix-up at the main office, and with Cannes being so busy with a big trade fair...'

Sadie could see that Leon was frowning a little, and so she offered calmingly, 'As there are only the two of us the size of the car doesn't really matter, does it?'

Leon took the keys from the receptionist and turned to smile warmly at her.

'Does having such a good nature come naturally to you, or do you have to work at it?' he teased her gently as he took her arm and guided her out into the warm morning sunshine.

Sadie cast him a wry look.

'You didn't give me the impression that you thought I had a good nature when we first met,' she reminded him dryly.

'Ah.' Leon gave her a droll look. 'But that was before.'

'Before what?' Sadie couldn't resist asking as he led her towards the small compact hire car parked just outside the main entrance.

Bending his head towards her, Leon replied wickedly, 'Before I kissed you.' He was playing with fire and he knew it, but suddenly he felt happier than he had felt in a long long time.

Speechlessly Sadie got into the passenger seat. Leon was quite definitely flirting with her, and somehow she didn't think that he was the type of man to flirt with every woman he met. No, when Leon flirted, it was because…

Because what? Because he wanted to idle away a few spare days enjoying a brief sexual liaison? Sadie shivered, as though the words 'brief' and 'liaison' were lumps of ice someone had dropped down her back.

It really was a compact car, she acknowledged ruefully a few minutes later, as she saw the way that Leon was practically folded over the steering wheel.

'In Australia we wouldn't give something of this size to our kids in case we were convicted of child abuse,' he told her in disgust as he inserted the key into the ignition.

Sadie laughed.

'I thought it was only Texas where everything was bigger than anywhere else,' she teased him, but her laughter turned into a small anxious frown as the car refused to start.

Cursing beneath his breath, Leon tried again—and this time, to Sadie's relief, the engine fired.

The farmhouse Leon was planning to rent for the summer was in the Massif de l'Estérel region of Provence, a beautiful mountainous area made up of the volcanic rock porphyry. The sides of the mountains were cloaked in forests of pine and cork oaks. Sadie felt a thrill of excitement at the thought of visiting such a beautiful area, and an even sharper one at the thought of visiting it with Leon.

However, because of some roadworks in the centre of Mougins they had to take a circuitous route in order to get to the road that would take them up into the region.

As they drove through the countryside surrounding Mougins Sadie couldn't resist pointing out to Leon the fields full of flowers grown for the perfume industry.

'How can anything made in a laboratory come anywhere near rivalling the scent of these?' she asked him passionately, gesturing towards fields of roses and jasmine.

'No, it doesn't,' Leon agreed with a glinting look towards her. 'For one thing with a chemically based scent there's no risk of the final product differing from batch to batch because the sun shone for three days less one year! And that means that when a woman buys a chemically created perfume she can be sure she is getting exactly the same scent that was in her previous bottle—and at an affordable price!'

Sadie's forehead puckered into a frown. From listening to Leon it would be easy to imagine that he had not changed his stance at all on the creation of the new perfume. Or was he simply trying to bait her?

She opened her mouth to vigorously defend her own stance, but Leon shook his head and gave her a meaningful look.

'Remember our pact?' he warned her.

Sadie laughed, but inwardly she couldn't help wishing that she could talk with him about her excitement and enthusiasm for her work on creating their new perfume. *Their* new perfume... She was also aching to get to work on the old-fashioned men's cologne produced by Francine, to update it, to make out of it a scent that was intensely male...a fragrance that would for ever and always be for her the mark of the man she was so passionately drawn to. Leon's scent...

Dreamily she let her imagination go to work! She would name it Leon—in her own secret thoughts if not in public—and it would be topaz-dark in hue, leonine, discreet, sensual, strong, earthy and rich, yet with a touch of coolness and hauteur, a fragrant suggestion of the pale green ice that was Leon's eyes! Leon…Leon… The bottle would be tall and round, wide enough for a man's hand to grip comfortably and feel at ease with…

Guiltily Sadie snatched her recklessly wayward thoughts back to reality.

Leon was an excellent driver in whose care she felt extremely safe, and she was pleased when he praised her map-reading skills and thanked her for finding them a shorter route to the motorway.

'I dare say this wretched slug of a car will mean that it will take us longer to get there than I had expected,' Leon warned her once they reached the right road. 'And heaven alone knows how it will cope with climbing the mountains.'

Sadie gave him a rueful look. Although he was complaining, he was not doing so in a bad-tempered manner, rather a wryly resigned one. It increased her growing respect for him to see that he could control his reaction to difficult situations.

In fact, as she was quickly discovering, time spent in Leon's company was such a blissful experience that merely sitting beside him inside a car made her feel happier than she suspected, as a sane modern woman, she had any right to be feeling.

As Leon had predicted, the small car laboured wretchedly up the steep mountain roads, but Sadie was too entranced by their surroundings and her companion to care. She had read in the guide book provided with the car that the porphyry rock that formed the mountains held colours which ranged from the deepest red in Cap Roux through to blue in Agay, where the Romans had made the column shafts for their monuments in Provence, to green, yellow, purple and grey. But to actually glimpse these rich colours through the deep green screen of the forest made her catch her breath in awe, unable to resist drawing Leon's attention to what she had seen.

'They are awesome,' he agreed, his expression deliberately teasing as he added, 'That is unless you have seen Ayers Rock!'

'Oh, you.' Sadie pulled a face at him and then stopped, her eyes misting a little with emotion as she realised how easy and natural she felt with him—just as though she had known him for years...

From somewhere deep inside her the words 'soul mates' rose up and would not be denied. Soul mate. Wasn't that truly what every single human being longed for? To meet their own one and only soul mate? To be with their special-once-in-a-lifetime person who was their fate and their destiny?

A tiny little shiver quivered through her.

'Cold?' Leon asked, frowning and reaching out to the air-conditioning control.

Sadie shook her head, but a small perverse part of her was pleased when he turned his head to give her a searching look, and then, and only then, seemed prepared to accept her statement. Ridiculously, she knew—given her age and the fact that she had looked after herself for so long—it gave her a tiny thrill of pleasure to know that he was so concerned for her comfort. Perhaps another woman might have accused him of being stereotypically male but Sadie admitted she was actually enjoying the sensation of being cared for.

'Does it look from the map as though it's much further?' Leon asked with a small frown as the car crawled up yet another steep hill.

Obligingly, Sadie checked the map. Ironically, it gave her as much pleasure to be treated as an equal partner in their shared venture as it had done only seconds ago to feel he regarded her as someone in need of his care and protection.

'Well, it's going on for twenty miles to the village you mentioned,' she told him.

'In that case we'd better stop for some lunch. Is there anywhere before then?' Leon asked.

'We should be coming up to a place called the Auberge des Adrets soon,' Sadie informed him, looking at the guidebook again. 'It was once supposed to be the favourite haunt of some highwayman named Gaspard de Besse. But there's a small town a little bit further on,' she added. 'Why don't we stop there and buy some food? Then we can eat when we get to the *mas*.'

When Leon shot her a surprised look Sadie back-pedalled a little, telling him, 'You said that it was un-occupied, so I thought in view of the time it's taking us to get there... But if you would rather eat at a restaurant...'

'No...buying our own stuff is fine by me. In fact I think it's a great idea,' Leon assured her immediately.

'Well, we should be reaching the town soon,' Sadie assured him.

Watching her as she concentrated on the guidebook, diligently checking that they were travelling in the right direction, Leon admitted that he could not think of a time when he had last enjoyed himself so much—couldn't remember a time when he had enjoyed a woman's company so much. Back home, the women he occasionally dated would have thrown a fit had he suggested taking them anywhere other than the most expensive and fashionable places to eat. And when he did, eating was the last thing they actually did.

They tended to parade up and down in their designer clothes, apply lipstick to their already vermilioned mouths whilst checking out the other occupants of the tables in their compact mirrors. They'd wave to their friends with long polished nails, whilst pouting complaints to him that they couldn't possibly drink anything other than the most expensive champagne. Oh, yes they did all that! But eat? Never!

Oh, they would certainly order the most expensive dishes on the menu, all right, but then refuse to eat them, protesting about calories and fat content. If there was one thing Leon hated it was seeing good food wasted—a hang-up from his upbringing, no doubt, when his grandmother had often regaled him with stories of how poor she and his grandfather had been, and how one joint of meat had been made to last a whole week.

Sadie wasn't like the spoiled society women he had previously dated, though. Last night and this morning she had eaten her food with every evidence of enjoyment. And somehow he found just watching her doing that far more sexually stirring than watching a stick-thin model-type toying irritably with a piece of designer greenery.

And surely a woman with a healthy appetite for food would have an equally healthy appetite for life's other sensual pleasures?

Leon recognised that his thoughts were about to surge dangerously out of control.

'I think the town is coming up now,' Sadie warned him

As he nodded his head in acknowledgement, Leon reflected ruefully that the town wasn't on its own!

*   *   *

'You've bought enough food to feed at least a dozen people.' Sadie laughed, shaking her head in mock disapproval as she and Leon headed back to the car. Both of them were carrying the purchases Leon had insisted on making.

He'd excitedly bought long sticks of French bread, freshly baked that morning, some local cheese and fruit, some olives, and some cold meats from the local *charcuterie*, some delicious delicacies from the patisserie, and even a bottle of red wine, as well as some water. It was a feast fit for any king

But Leon wasn't a king, he was a billionaire, Sadie reminded herself as they reached the car. No wonder he had looked at her in such surprise when she had suggested they buy food and virtually picnic at the *mas*.

'What's wrong?' Leon demanded, making her jump as she realised that he was watching her.

The genuine concern in his voice and the perceptiveness of the look he was giving her brought Sadie to a standstill in the middle of the empty street.

'Sadie?'

The intensity with which Leon spoke her name as he raised one hand to her face, gently tucking an errant strand of hair behind her ear, caused Sadie to tremble from head to foot, the paper bag she was clutching in her arms shaking with her.

Very gently Leon's hand stroked down the side of her head, before resting on her neck, his thumb massaging the delicate flesh just behind her ear in a way, to judge from the concerned look in his eyes, Sadie suspected he had intended to be comforting and reassuring, but in fact was anything but. Her whole body leapt into shocking, aroused life immediately, her tremors increasing.

What on earth must Leon think of her? He must be used to sophisticated, experienced woman who did not react like inexperienced and over-excited teenagers the moment he touched them. Inexperienced…

Sadie pulled her mind back from the word like a mother protectively pulling a child's fingers back from an open flame.

Leon's hand was still cupping the side of her head, and somehow Sadie managed to make herself look directly into his eyes.

The look in their deep, deep depths was making her feel dizzy, holding her in thrall.

'Have I told you, yet, Sadie, just what a very exceptional person I think you are?'

Exceptional? Her? Sadie tried to remind herself of who he was and why she was with him, but the slow, gentle movement of his hand against her scalp was overheating her thoughts as well as her body. Beneath her clothes she could feel it reacting to him, her breasts filling with liquid aching need, her nipples tightening, flaunting their desire as they pushed hungrily against the fine silk of her bra. Low down in her stomach her muscles tightened, whilst the female core of her swelled and moistened.

Tiny beads of perspiration dampened her hairline and upper lip—and they were not caused by the heat of the sun, Sadie noted ruefully as she made a valiant attempt to behave as though she was perfectly accustomed to such a situation.

Leon looked closely at her as the soft, incredibly long dark lashes concealed Sadie's eyes from him. He could feel the tiny convulsive tremors of her body. They ran through his fingertips and up his arm, and from there right the whole way through him, to every last inch and single cell of him. He had never ever met a woman who made him feel like this, who aroused in him such a complex tangle of emotions and desires.

Within the space of a single heartbeat she could send him from the most intense physical need he could ever remember feeling to the most protective and tender realisation of just how vulnerable she was. In one breath she could make him want to be both poacher and gamekeeper. Right now, here in this hot little street, he could quite easily lean her against the nearest wall and take her in the most primitive, hungry male way there was—yes, and make her ache with the need he felt for every single heartbeat. But at the same time he also wanted to wrap a cloak of protection around her that would prevent any male eyes from ever looking lustfully on her, any male desire from ever hurting her.

Including his own?

Leon had never met a woman who made him feel that so much in life that was simple and easily affordable was somehow also invaluably pleasurable. Apart, perhaps, from his grandmother, She had also relished the simple and inexpensive things in life.

Suddenly Sadie pulled away from him.

Looking down at her, Leon growled. 'Do you have any idea how very, very tempted I am to kiss you?'

Sadie granted herself ten wonderful seconds in which to absorb the blissful delight that hearing these words gave her, and then another ten just because it felt so good. Then, in case she dangerously gave away how shamelessly she wanted him to kiss her, she turned away from him and started to hurry to where they had parked the car.

Leon watched her. He could still feel the warmth of her neat, delicately shaped head on his palm, the softness of her hair and her skin. As she walked away from him he watched the awesome femaleness in the movement of her body with male appreciation—and a very physical male response—only just managing to suppress a small growl of possessiveness as he contemplated the effect of her neatly rounded derrière on other vulnerable members of his sex who were witnessing it as she walked past them.

It was his duty, surely, to protect them from such vulnerability—and the temptation which accompanied it! For the sake of his own sex, Sadie needed a man in her life and a ring on her finger! A ring? His ring?

Now, where the hell had that thought come from?

They had to call at the local garage before leaving the town, to put more petrol in the car, and Leon frowned as he saw the way the driver of a car on the other side of the pumps paused to give Sadie a lingeringly appreciative second look before getting back into his vehicle.

'Seems like you've made a conquest,' he commented dryly to Sadie as he put the key in the ignition.

'It's probably my hair,' she answered matter-of-factly. She had already noticed how often local men looked at her blonde locks.

'Yeah, and the rest,' she thought she heard Leon mutter beneath his breath. But as she turned to look at him she realised that the car was as it had been this morning, when Leon had first attempted to start it—refusing to start!

Sadie held her breath as he tried again, and then again, To her relief, on the fourth attempt the engine fired.

CHAPTER SIX

HALF an hour later Sadie looked out of the passenger window and caught her first glimpse of the sea, way, way down below them—foam-capped, blue-green, dipping to denser all-blue where it met the horizon.

Automatically she gave a small exclamation of pleasure.

'Want a closer look?' Leon offered, moving to pull over to the side of the road, where there was a convenient parking space.

Sadie was tempted, but she knew that it was taking them much longer to reach the *mas* than Leon had expected. If they were to stop she knew she would also be tempted to look for a path down the steep cliff, so that she could sink her toes into the untouched golden sand of the small, perfect half-moon-shaped beach which was just visible below them. And of course once on that beach she would definitely need to at least dip her feet into the sea itself!

The thought of the two of them sharing the privacy of that small beach, even perhaps picnicking there, with the food they had bought, made her long to accept Leon's suggestion. Sternly she reminded herself of the reason they were here, and the fact that that she was an adult and not a child.

Leon was still waiting for her to reply. Regretfully, she shook her head.

Recognising the wistfulness in her expression, Leon twitched his mouth in amusement. But, like her, he was conscious of how long the journey was taking them. At this rate they would no sooner have reached the *mas* than it would be time to turn back! Nevertheless... The thought of being alone with Sadie on that small deserted beach was a very tempting one. A very, very tempting one indeed!

Deliberately suppressing it, he put his foot down a little harder on the accelerator. The small car struggled to respond, chugging valiantly up the steep incline.

'Not much further now,' Leon assured Sadie as they turned off the coast road and onto a narrower road which would take them to the *mas*.

About ten minutes after leaving that road, and driving down a private lane, they found it. A small cosy spread of red-roofed, warmth-washed buildings, perched halfway up the hillside and facing out to sea.

Leon brought the car to a halt outside it, and neither of them spoke as they both gazed at the *mas*.

Without a word Leon pressed the automatic buttons and opened their car windows—as though he had guessed what she was thinking, Sadie reflected as she breathed in the wonderfully pure air. Even up here, at this height, she would have sworn she could smell and taste the sea.

Lavender shrubs scented the air with their flowers, and the silvery-grey trunk of a wisteria leaned heavily against the golden walls of the *mas*, its branches covered in soft feathery leaves. A scattering of obviously self-seeded semi-wild flowers threw up their heads in warm bursts of colour that broke up the green of the grass, and beyond the *mas* Sadie could see a small olive grove. But what really caught her eye was the low wall, bordered with an informal hedge of orange trees, beyond which she could see the enticing sparkle of water. The *mas* had a swimming pool! And not just any swimming pool, but one of the stunning modern infinity pools that had recently become so fashionable. From where she was looking, it really did seem as though the water in the pool actually merged with the sea, so that the sparkling blue water seemed to stretch into infinity.

The whole place combined a perfect blend of traditional and modern design, Sadie recognised. If this place was hers she knew there was no way she could ever bear to let it to anyone else.

'Oh, how beautiful!' Her soft, delighted words broke the silence and had Leon turning his head to look at her.

'This is the first time I've actually seen it.' His voice sounded gruff and slightly hoarse, as though he was as affected by the wild, private beauty of the *mas* as she was herself, but trying in a manlike way to hide it. 'In the flesh, I mean,' he amended. 'The agent sent me photographs and a video. I told him I wanted somewhere private, and this place is certainly that.'

'It's heavenly,' Sadie told him, so caught up in the spell of the place that she had opened the car door and stepped out without even realising she had done so.

A soft breeze stroked over her skin and instinctively she held her face up to the sun, closing her eyes as she basked in its warmth.

Turning to Leon, and gesturing widely with her arms to encompass the *mas*, the land and the sea and sky beyond it, she told him huskily, 'This is what perfume is all about—flowers, earth, air, sea, capturing the scents of nature. No laboratory-produced chemical can ever reproduce this!' she finished passionately.

Sombrely Leon watched her. The breeze was moulding her clothes to her body, highlighting its curves. He was tempted to challenge her statement, to remind her that she herself had now agreed to work with man-made scents, but he was reluctant to introduce a note of conflict into their day. In her eyes he could see how intensely she felt, and irrevocably he knew that he wanted to share that passion and, dangerously, he wanted *her*.

'Let's take a look inside.'

The harshness of Leon's voice made Sadie frown. Had he thought her foolish and over-emotional to feel the way she did about their surroundings? He was waiting for her, and so silently she fell into step beside him.

Inside, the *mas* was every bit as perfect as it was outside—at least in Sadie's opinion. The large country-style kitchen opened out onto a shady secluded patio, complete with a family-sized table and chairs, the patio itself ornamented with tubs of geraniums and an old-fashioned water pump.

The long, sprawling building also housed a cosy TV room, as well as a formal dining room and a wonderfully large and elegant sitting room, which ran the full width of the house and had windows on either side.

Upstairs there were five good-sized bedroom, each with its own bathroom. Every room was furnished simply but with style. With each step she took Sadie found herself envying whoever it was who owned it—especially when Leon told her that the land attached to the *mas* extended right down to the sea and included its own private beach.

'It's absolutely wonderful,' she told him.

'You like it?'

'How could anyone not?' Sadie responded ruefully. 'If it was mine, I don't think I could bear to let it out to someone else.'

As soon as she had finished speaking Leon found that he was actually making mental plans to get in touch with the letting agent and find out if the owners would be prepared to sell! After all, it would make sense for him to have a permanent base in Europe—especially now that they were taking over Francine.

Come off it, he derided himself. That isn't why you want it, and you damn well know it. No. It wasn't himself, dressed in a business suit and working alone on his laptop, he was envisaging. It was he and Sadie, and what they were doing had nothing whatsoever to do with work or laptops!

'Well, I don't know about you, but I am ready for that food we bought,' Leon told Sadie, hastily banishing his wayward thoughts. He looked at his watch and added ruefully, 'Do you realise that it's already half past three?'

Sadie hadn't realised, as she had been far too entranced by the house to think about the time.

'Where would you like to eat? Inside or out?' Leon asked her.

'Oh, outside—if that's okay with you?' Sadie responded immediately.

'By the pool?' Leon guessed.

Sadie gave him an eloquent look of confirmation, her eyes shining with pleasure. Watching her, Leon didn't know how the hell he was managing to stop himself from taking hold of her and kissing her until that look of shining pleasure became one of liquid desire.

'It's a pity we didn't bring our swimming things,' Sadie regretted innocently, as she looked longingly at the pool.

'Who says we need them?' Leon teased her softly, laughing outright as he saw her expression.

'What? Don't tell me you've never been skinny-dipping?' He grinned in disbelief. 'You live by the sea, don't you?'

Sadie shook her head vehemently.

'I certainly have not,' she told him firmly, but the expression in her eyes was a little wistful.

The mere thought of swimming naked with Leon in the soft warm water of the pool was sending her imagination into definitely x-rated regions, and making her pulse bounce excitement though her body. Protectively, she hid her reaction from Leon. Her grandmother had been of a generation that believed that it was a man's role to pursue a woman, most definitely not the woman's to pursue him. And although Sadie knew such teachings were outmoded now, a little bit of her still clung to them. Perhaps it was as a consequence of that that her own sexual experience was rather limited—or at least she suspected that in Leon's eyes it would be.

'I was brought up by my grandmother, remember,' she defended, when she saw his expression. 'And besides,' she added dryly, 'the water off the coast of Pembroke is extremely cold.'

Ten minutes later, as they unpacked the food which Leon had brought from the kitchen where they had stored it, Sadie realised just how hungry she was.

'No, thanks,' she refused, shaking her head and covering the wine glass Leon had found as he reached for the wine he had bought.

He raised his eyebrows and teased her. 'Why not? Are you afraid that it might weaken your grandmother-induced resolve enough for you to want to try skinny-dipping after all?'

He was just teasing her. Sadie knew that. After all, he couldn't know how much she wanted him...

Refusing to rise to his bait, she firmly dismissed the tormenting erotic images from her mind and told him calmly, 'You can't have any wine because you're driving, and I don't want to drink any without you. It doesn't seem fair.'

The look she could see in his eyes as he replaced the bottle and reached for one of water instead confused her.

As he poured them both a glass of water, Leon noted that Sadie was constantly surprising and challenging not only his original assessment of her, but also his understanding of women in general. In refusing to drink any wine because he could not share in the pleasure she had shown a genuine kindness of nature which he admitted was seriously denting the barriers he had felt he needed to put up against her. Denting it? Get real, he advised himself derisively. She had damn near demolished it wholesale!

'Mmm…those olives look good,' Leon commented hungrily as he watched Sadie opening the small carton containing them.

'Want one?' she responded immediately, picking one up without thinking about the sensual intimacy of her action as she offered to feed it to him.

The look he gave her made her suddenly conscious of the heat prickling on her back, and even more aware of the heat trickling through her body. She hadn't meant to be provocative, but right now the way he was looking at her made her feel as though she were Eve, offering Adam that apple!

However, before she could retract either her words or the olive, Leon's hand snaked out and his fingers curled softly around her wrist, making her heart bounce around inside her chest as though it were on a piece of elastic. How could such a small gesture, such a simple touch, have such a powerful and erotic effect upon her? She might not be sexually experienced, but she wasn't totally naïve! Somewhere at the back of her mind the knowledge surfaced that a part of her had known from the minute she had set eyes on him that Leon was going to affect her like this.

Dizzily she noted how cool Leon's hold was, and how potentially strong. Her wrist felt so fragile in his grip. She could feel his thumb pressing against her pulse-point and her heart gave a violently convulsive jerk.

Without her even wanting it, never mind being able to do a thing to stop him, Leon had lifted her hand to his mouth. Her eyes rounded, their colour darkening as her gaze followed his every movement. Helplessly, she watched as his lips parted, encompassing not just the juicy pitted black olive but her fingertips as well.

Her own lips parted involuntarily, her mouth going dry as a fierce ache burst into life inside her.

The sensation of Leon's tongue curling over her fingers and then thrusting between to remove the olive made her go light-headed with desire. Her heart was pumping as ferociously as though she had just run up a steep mountainside. Shockingly explicit images were forming inside her head, and waves of liquid desire were shafting through her body like bolts of lightning. The thumb pressed so close to her pulse must surely be registering its erratic beat.

The olive had gone from her fingers, but Leon's tongue had not! It was lapping slowly and surely, with deliberate sensuality, at her flesh, removing the satin covering of olive oil.

'Mmm,' she heard Leon whisper throatily, glancing up into her eyes as he did so and giving her a wicked look. 'Very more-ish!'

Sadie's eyes opened wide and her face turned a vivid

shade of pink. He wasn't, she suspected, referring to the olive!

His tongue laved her fingers one more time with lingering thoroughness, and then he lifted his head to look at her, whilst his hand slid down over her wrist to cover hers, folding her fingers into her palm and slowly stroking her small fist as he asked her softly, 'Are you sure you don't want a glass of wine?'

Emphatically Sadie shook her head and tried to repossess her hand. She was intoxicated enough as it was, without drinking wine! The sensuality of what he had done had sent her blood into a cloud of fizzy bubbles as it raced round her veins.

Watching her, Leon was instinctively and sharply aware of her sexual naïveté, and that knowledge sent a huge reactionary surge of corresponding male arousal thundering through him.

He had never been promiscuous, but naturally as a young man he had gone through the normal stages of sexual experimentation and exploration. Since hitting his late twenties, though, he had given up on sexual exploration as a means of expressing himself as a man. However, the majority of women he met were very open about the fact that they were extremely sexually experienced. They seemed to think that he would enjoy the results of that experience. Perhaps like Sadie he had been imbued with a lot of his own grandmother's moral beliefs.

There was also, Leon acknowledged, enough Greek heritage in him to make him find such women more of a turn-off than a turn-on. His realisation that Sadie was clearly quite inexperienced was producing within him the same effect as applying a lighted match to dry tinder—very dry tinder, he recognised grimly.

Whether it was unacceptable in today's modern climate or not, there was something within him, something in his blood, that found the knowledge that there would be much he would have the pleasure of showing her extremely attractive! Extremely attractive and insistently arousing, as his body was making very, very plain!

He was delighted that potentially they had the summer ahead of them to get to know one another. He would make it his business to be sure he spent as much time in France as he could, and he would see to it that Sadie also needed to be there, for constant 'consultations' regarding the new perfume she would be creating for them.

Still watching her, he discovered that he was toying with ways and means of re-vamping the Grasse house and outbuildings, and insisting that it was essential that Sadie worked from there on the perfume.

That way their relationship could grow easily and naturally, and when they came to make a full commitment to one another it would be—

A full commitment?

Leon underwent a moment of wry introspection and self-searching. He was Greek enough to feel very strongly that he only wanted to make a full commitment to one woman and for that partnership to be for ever. And he was modern-minded enough to know that that kind of commitment couldn't be based solely on sexual and emotional desire, but had to be based on mutual trust, honesty and respect as well.

He had met too many women who were ready to say anything to get what they wanted. No way could he ever give his love and his life to a woman like that!

As he looked at Sadie he was uncomfortably aware that whilst his thoughts might be logical and under control, his feelings and his body were no such thing. The way he was feeling right now meant that the sooner they left the *mas* the better! The combination of Sadie, solitude and his own sexual longing for her right now were putting his self-control under far too much strain!

With that in mind, he stood up, frowning.

What was Leon thinking? Sadie wondered, watching him uncertainly. Two minutes ago he had been behaving towards her in a way that had quite definitely been very sexual. Now he was looking at her with a sternness that seemed to suggest she had done something wrong!

Perhaps he thought she had been deliberately provocative?

She quickly got to her feet herself, her pleasure in the day flattened by Leon's expression.

'I think it's time we made a move,' Leon announced grimly, adding under his breath so that Sadie couldn't hear him, 'Before it's too late!'

'You want us to leave now?' Sadie couldn't stop herself from questioning in disbelief. And then, when Leon made no response, she protested crossly, 'It might have escaped your notice, but I haven't had anything to eat yet.'

'You can eat in the car,' Leon told her unequivocally, bending down to pick up the bottle of wine as he did so.

The sky above them was still cloudlessly blue, the sea in the distance a deeper but just as storm-free hue. The lightest of breezes stirred the flowers, and the only sound on the clear air was the lazy hum of bees. So why did Sadie suddenly feel as though a very dangerous and threatening storm was imminent? she wondered miserably. Why did she feel as though the sky had turned dark and the coldest of icy winds was piercing her heart? Why?

Did she really need to ask herself that? she questioned

herself derisively whilst she stared at Leon's departing back as he walked towards the car. If ever a man's back was indicative of tightly reined in anger and cold savagery, then that back was Leon's!

Why on earth hadn't she had the sense to think first, before stupidly, idiotically, senselessly offering him that olive? Her face burned a self-contemptuous red. Of course he was bound to have thought she was coming on to him! But if he had thought that then why hadn't he simply rejected her immediately? Why on earth had he deliberately emphasised the sensuality of the moment in the way that he had? Had it been her own lack of experience that had put him off? Sadie wasn't entirely unfamiliar with the type of man who valued a woman purely on her sexual experience and availability, but naïvely she had believed that Leon was far above that kind of thing!

After a brief visit to the bathroom, to prepare herself for the journey and to reinforce to herself all the reasons why she should cease to feel anything whatsoever for Leon, she was ready to join him in the car.

Pulling on her seat beat, she remained resolutely silent as Leon moved to start the car—and continued to be so during the five unsuccessful attempts that followed the first.

However, when Leon finally unlocked the bonnet and got out, lifting it up to peer into the innards of the vehicle, Sadie felt anxious enough to ask, 'What is it? What's wrong?'

'God knows,' came back Leon's terse response. 'I'm no mechanic, but I suspect it's the battery. I'm going to have to ring the car hire people and get them to sort something out for us.'

Leon snapped the bonnet closed and came back to the car to get his mobile phone.

Five minutes later Sadie held her breath as she heard Leon demand ominously into his mobile, 'What do you mean, you can't supply me with a substitute?'

There was a brief pause before he cut in acidly, 'Look, I don't give a damn how busy you are, or how impossible it is for you to get a car out here to me until tomorrow. I would have thought any organisation that considered itself as anything approaching professional would have had the common sense to make sure it had enough vehicles to cover this extra busy period. Hell!' he swore bitterly as he held the instrument away from his ear. 'The line's breaking up,' he told Sadie grimly.

They tried to contact the hire firm on three successive occasions, both with Leon's mobile and Sadie's, and eventually managed to get through. But once again the hire car firm insisted that they were not able to provide Leon with a substitute vehicle until the following morning.

'Well, at least we've got the *mas* to stay in,' Sadie pointed out.

Leon was staring grimly out to sea.

'Yeah, great,' he agreed nastily

The toxicity of his silence was burning Sadie's sensitive nerve-endings.

'Look, I can see that you don't want to be here with me—' she began.

'For heaven's sake, Sadie.' Leon stopped her savagely. 'Don't you understand? It isn't what I *don't* want that's bothering me. It's what I *do* want.'

Sadie's forehead crinkled with her lack of understanding.

'I can see that you want to get back,' she began warily, 'but I don't—'

Leon groaned.

'No, Sadie!' he interrupted bluntly. 'What I want isn't to get back—although hell knows it damn well ought to be. What I want is you!'

His angry words seemed to hang in the enclosed space of the car, reverberating in her ears.

Her? He wanted her?

Sadie tried to say something, but her throat was too dry and the words stuck there. She swallowed and managed to squeak, 'You want me? But—'

'Yes. I want you!' Leon confirmed thickly. 'Every damned intoxicating, aggravating, delicious, sensual inch of you,' he ground out in fierce despair.

Head spinning, Sadie wondered at the strength of the feeling gripping her. What would Leon say if she told him that she fully reciprocated? What would he do?

'Have you any idea just what kind of hell it's going to be for me, having to spend the night here with you— alone. Just the two of us!' Leon emphasised tightly. 'Just the two of us!'

When she didn't say anything, he demanded harshly, 'Didn't last night tell you anything? Show you? Warn you. I could hardly keep my hands off you then!'

Sadie had had enough.

'Would it be such a terrible thing if you didn't?' she asked him bravely.

Leon stared at her, expression on his face hardening his eyes glittering green fire.

'I'm going to pretend I didn't hear that,' he told her grittily.

Sadie wasn't going to give in—no way, not now!

'Why?' she challenged him softly

'Why?'

She could hear raw anger in his voice, threaded with disbelief.

'I can't believe you're asking me that,' he told her flatly. 'I mean, you do know what I'm talking about, don't you? I'm a man, Sadie, and to put it in its bluntest terms, if I come anywhere near you feeling like I do right now... Wanting you like I do right now... Hell, Sadie, all it would take would be just for me to smell the scent of you, never mind touch you! And if I did touch you—'

The look of male hunger he was giving her made Sadie quiver from head to foot!

Grimly he continued, 'Well, let's just say I can't pretend that I am going to be able to stop at a few kisses this time.'

Sadie took a deep breath. Life was offering her an opportunity, and she realised she wanted to seize it with both hands. Right now she couldn't think of anything she wanted more than to make love with Leon. To touch him! Breathe him! Know him in every way that there was! What she was thinking...feeling...wanting...shocked her— but it excited her as well, she admitted.

Leon didn't look excited, though; far from it! The green glacier look was back in his eyes, sending her heart to a thudding drumbeat of a standstill.

How could he speak to her in the way he just had? How could he say the things he just had? How could he make her feel the way he just had and then look at her with that cold iciness in his eyes?

'Look, let's not mince matters,' Leon told her harshly. 'I don't go in for immediate sexual gratification, or casual sex, and before you try to tell me anything different I'm damn sure you don't either!'

Casual sex! Sadie could feel the raw acid taste of her

own shocked pain. It swamped her in a savage wave that tensed her whole body and washed the colour from her face.

Instinctively she wanted to hide what she was feeling from Leon, but somehow she just couldn't find the strength to turn away from him. She could feel her skin prickling with awareness as he looked at her.

When Leon saw Sadie's revealing expression he cursed under his breath and pushed his hand through his hair.

'We've both got one hell of a lot going on in our lives right now,' he told her brusquely. 'I want you, Sadie. Make no mistake about that. But, hell, Sadie,' he swore, when she continued to look at him with an open expression of anguished pain in her eyes, 'can't you see that I'm trying my hardest to protect you? Can't you see that I'm struggling to do the decent thing? Feeling the way I do right now...wanting you the way I do right now...' He groaned. 'Having to spend the night alone here with you is the last thing I need.'

Sadie told herself that she wouldn't have been a woman if she hadn't felt a very satisfying spurt of sensual pleasure at Leon's admission. Far more dangerous, though, was the even stronger surge of excitement that speared through her, and the knowledge that, high-minded though Leon's intentions were, an unexpectedly wicked part of her was strongly tempted to put them to the test. In the hope that they failed!

Hastily she looked away from him, in case that all-seeing gaze of his might somehow guess what she was thinking. Thoroughly bemused by what she was feeling, Sadie shrugged her shoulders and told Leon huskily, 'Well, no matter what either of us feels about it, we don't have any alternative. We are going to have to spend the night here!'

There—that should hopefully convince him that she wasn't secretly pleased that they were going to be here together alone…

'Sadie, I give you my word that you'll be perfectly safe,' Leon told her rawly.

As she turned away from him and started to walk back towards the *mas*, Sadie admitted to herself that she wasn't at all sure that 'safe' was what she wanted to be. In fact she knew that it wasn't! Not when the alternative was a blissful night spent in Leon's arms, enjoying and exploring Leon's body, having him explore hers…all of hers, with his hands and his mouth and…

Guiltily Sadie quickened her step as her whole body melted on a wave of unstoppable longing. Leon would be a wonderful lover. Somehow she already knew that. And her body wanted him to be its lover—*wanted* him to be! She had to stand still as her body reacted to her thoughts with a shocking surge of need.

Watching her, Leon discovered to his chagrin that he was actually grinding his teeth in frustration as a surge of hot male hunger gripped him. Fiercely he tried to resist the impulse to remember how she had felt in his arms last night when he had kissed her. He had given Sadie his word that he wouldn't touch her, and he fully intended to keep it!

Briefly he looked away from her, battling against himself when he discovered that his body was telling him very determinedly and openly just how much it opposed what he had decided.

Already it was tormenting him with dangerous thoughts and even more dangerous images of what it would feel like to share the pleasure of love with Sadie, of what it would be like to share the heat of desire with her, and the intimacy of knowing one another's bodies!

God, but he wanted her, Leon realised savagely—which was exactly why he would have given anything, paid anything, not to have to spend the night here at the *mas* with her.

He was a man of honour, and seducing her...

Seducing her. Leon leaned against the car and gave in to the fierce tide of heat that ripped through him.

He would undress her slowly, uncovering her inch by inch, touching her, stroking her, reassuring her as he kissed the soft sweetness of her skin, her throat, and that delicate delicious spot just behind her ear, her jaw, her eyelids and then her mouth.

Leon closed his eyes and tried to fight the surge of arousal engulfing him. But it was impossible. He could feel the immediate stiffening of his body and cursed himself beneath his breath, relieved that Sadie was too far away from him to be aware of his reaction.

But even knowing what his thoughts were doing wasn't enough to stop them. Not now...

He would kiss Sadie slowly and chastely, waiting until she was ready for the intimate exploration of his tongue. Somehow he would find a way to control his need to thrust it hotly into the sweetness of her mouth. And then, once she had accepted him there, he would start to explore her body, the delicate curve of her arm just above her elbow, the inside of her wrist, the soft slope of her neck where it met her shoulder. And her breasts...

Leon felt the fierce thrusting reaction of his own body, saw when he looked down where his erection strained against the cloth of his jeans. Inside them he was hard and aching, so tumescent that it hurt.

Sadie had already reached the *mas*. He knew he ought

to follow her, but his need for her was devouring him—and if he did...if he even got within breathing distance of her right now, never mind close enough to touch her, Leon knew that he wouldn't be able to trust himself to keep the promise he had made to her.

Just the thought of cupping the soft weight of her breasts in his hands, of exploring them, running his fingertip around that place where the creamy paleness gave way to the deeper pinkness of her aureole before rising up to the nipple itself, was sending him crazy with longing.

His erection throbbed and pulsed. Inside his head, his hand was already travelling down her body, stroking her thighs, easing them apart, exploring the soft warmth of the full swollen lips protecting her sex with gentle reassurance before sliding between them to probe the moist excitement of her, and then...

Leon groaned out aloud and sliced a mental guillotine down across his thoughts. If he continued like this he wouldn't be able to walk as far as the house, never mind do anything else, he told himself grittily.

He didn't just want Sadie, he admitted angrily. He damn well loved her as well!

And loving her meant that he wanted to protect her. Not just from any other man who might dare to take advantage of her, but from himself!

He was in this so deep he might as well give up right now, Leon admitted. But he couldn't afford to. Not until he had got the takeover sorted.

He was glad that Sadie had seen sense with regard to his plans for Francine. His board would not have been too pleased, to say the least, had he had to institute potentially expensive and—even worse—long drawn-out legal proceedings against Sadie to prove that the Myrrh perfume formula belonged legally to Francine. He needed that formula, Leon admitted, and he needed it badly—because he wanted to make good the vow he had made in his grandmother's name and memory: that women the world over would be able to enjoy and afford the perfume she had so longed for as a young woman.

When that had been done he could give himself time to court Sadie, and to love her. Not until then. And right now he had the night to get through!

At least they weren't going to starve whilst they waited for their replacement vehicle. Thanks to Sadie. Leon closed his eyes, reliving that moment when she had handed him the olive. An innocent Eve, indeed!

His erection stiffened and once again he muttered an imprecation under his breath. He was thirty-four years old, for heaven's sake, and well past the age when he ought to be getting a hard-on just thinking about sex.

But he wasn't just thinking about sex. He was thinking about Sadie! And he was thinking about love! Thinking about it. Aching for it—and for Sadie!

CHAPTER SEVEN

IT WAS gone eleven o'clock. In the kitchen of the *mas*, Sadie suppressed a small yawn and cast a wary look at Leon.

They had eaten a meal together earlier in the evening, and Leon had once again refused any of the wine—although why he should have done so Sadie had no idea, since he was not going to be driving after all.

She had had some, though! To give her the resilience to get through the evening? To help her to block out the savage and aching longing driving through her, urging her to take the kind of provocative sexual action she would normally not just have totally deplored but refused to even consider? Her? Seduce Leon? Her brain said no way, but her emotions and her body ached. If only...

Luckily, all the beds in the *mas* possessed bedclothes, and Leon had managed to turn on the hot water, so at least she would be able to have a shower before she went to bed.

A shelf of books in the TV room should have provided her with some means of passing the time and removing herself from Leon's presence, but stubbornly, and with alcohol-underpinned courage, she had refused to do so, remaining instead in the kitchen even though it was now over two hours since they had finished eating.

'You're tired,' Leon announced in a clipped voice. 'Why don't you go to bed?'

Why didn't she remove her unwanted company from his presence was more like it, Sadie reflected bitterly, but she kept her thoughts to herself as she smothered another yawn. She *was* tired, she admitted, but strangely she was reluctant to leave the kitchen.

Strangely? Since when had it been remotely strange for a woman in love to want to leave the company of the man she loved? Sadie derided herself mentally.

A woman in love? She was in love with Leon? Well, wasn't she? *Wasn't* she?

All right, she admitted angrily. All right! But that didn't mean…

That didn't mean what? she questioned herself mercilessly. That didn't mean that right now she just ached to leave her chair and go over to him and wrap her arms around him? To kiss her way all along his jaw and tease her fingers through his hair? She wanted to taste the texture of his skin and explore the deliciously tempting outline of his mouth, whilst her free hand tugged his tee shirt out of his jeans and slid beneath it to feel the male strength of his chest, and then—

Frantically Sadie fought to reign in her rioting thoughts! Her face was burning, she knew, and no wonder. Perhaps it might be wiser if she *did* go to bed!

'You're right,' she told Leon huskily. 'I am tired. I will go to bed.'

Yes, she needed to get away from him before her body went totally out of control with longing and she ended up making a grab for him and putting her wanton thoughts into action!

Defiantly, she poured herself another glass of wine and picked it up. She had lied about being tired. She was far too wound up emotionally for sleep, but perhaps the wine would help her to do so.

Leon exhaled his pent-up breath in a savage sigh as he watched Sadie walk away from him. Morning couldn't come fast enough for him. How the hell was he supposed to do anything so mundane as sleep when he knew that Sadie was lying there in the next room?

No way was he tired yet. He decided he would walk round the gardens of the *mas* and try and get his feelings under control.

Gathering up the underwear she had rinsed out, Sadie padded naked from the bathroom to the bedroom. The *mas* was certainly well equipped, and she was enjoying the luxury it provided. She envied Leon his stay here.

She found she couldn't get Leon out of her head as she restlessly prowled around the bedroom, the glass of wine forgotten. And besides, a mere glass of wine wasn't capable of subduing her longing…her love…

Leon stared back towards the *mas*. Sadie would be in bed by now. The savagery of the need that gripped him tensed his jaw. He could see the swimming pool, the water shimmering in the moonlight. His body needed cooling down and his thoughts needed exorcising!

He reached the side of the pool in a few strides, stripping off his clothes by the edge, and launching himself into a neat dive that sliced the water almost silently.

A fierce front crawl took him the length of the pool and back.

Still wide awake, Sadie went to her bedroom window. It looked out onto the pool area of the garden, and her whole body stiffened as she saw Leon in the water.

She watched him for several seconds before going into her bathroom and pulling on the bathrobe she had found there.

Like a sleepwalker she opened her bedroom door and made her way quietly and purposefully through the *mas*.

When she reached the pool, Leon was swimming towards the opposite side. Calmly she took off the robe and left it beside the pool. Unlike Leon, she did not dive into the pool, preferring instead to slide her body into its deliciously warm water.

She was a good swimmer. Her stroke was perhaps not as powerful as Leon's, but still very accomplished and sleek, and it carried her speedily through the water to where Leon was just executing his turn.

She could see the look in his eyes as she reached him and put her feet down on the tiled floor of the pool. Here at the shallow end the water was just lapping the lower curves of her breasts, nudging erotically at her nipples before retreating to expose them fully, its touch a sensually warm caress that heightened her already aroused senses.

'Sadie—'

She could hear the harsh warning in his voice but she ignored it. Up above them the sky was a midnight-blue cover sprinkled with brilliant white diamond stars. Sea and pool merged into a shimmering infinity, reflecting the brilliance of the moon. Nightscape lighting had turned the gardens of the *mas* into a place of mystery and fantasy.

The only sound to disturb the warm silence were the lap of the water and their own breathing. Leon's was measured, but harsh, as though he was fighting to control it, and her own was so rapid with excitement that it was making her feel almost faint. Leon was standing up in the water, with his back against the tiles, and Sadie could see his expression quite clearly. He looked, she thought giddily, like some Greek god come to life, with his dark hair and strong chiselled features. And his body… Her heart did a dangerous slalom from what felt like a great height, and then skidded to a thudding halt against her ribs.

Leon's body, she admitted, gulping in air, was just the most sexy male body she had ever seen in her life! She had thought that bodies like Leon's only came courtesy of a Michaelangelo or a Leonardo. His torso was a perfect V shape, his shoulders impressively broad, his chest solid but not overly muscled, tapering into his waist. She itched to spread her fingers across his chest and to savour the silky warmth of the soft darkness of his body hair. Her heated gaze dropped helplessly to where the narrow line of hair disappeared beneath the water. Like her, he was naked…

Sadie could feel her breasts swelling and her nipples tightening. Her body quivered, agitating the water around her. Unable to stop herself, she moved closer to Leon and silently raised one trembling hand to his body.

'Sadie.' Leon's low-voiced growl warned her of her danger, but she refused to stop. The pleasure of touching him was going to her head like champagne.

She took another step closer and then pressed both her hands flat against his chest. Lifting her head, she touched her tongue-tip to the hollow at the base of his throat, savouring the hot, salt male taste of him.

Lost in what she was doing, she didn't see the storm signals or smell the dangerous scent of brimstone in the air. One minute she was standing in front of Leon, shivering with the knowledge that all that was keeping them apart was the soft surge of the water whilst her lips closed on the fierce pulse in his throat, and the next she was literally being imprisoned by Leon's arms as they wrapped themselves punishingly around her and his curses rang savagely in her ears.

'Are you crazy?' she heard him demanding furiously. 'Do you know what you're doing? Do you think I'm made of stone?'

Stone... No, of course not. Leon was all wonderful gorgeous, sexy, woman-arousing, hunky maleness, all hard muscles and solid flesh, excitingly scored with that enticing line of hair that her fingers just ached to explore, Sadie decided feverishly.

She wasn't even aware that she had spoken her thoughts out loud until she felt Leon's teeth nip sharply at her ear and heard him tell her rawly, 'That's it. You've just sent my self-control into lunar orbit. Hell, Sadie!'

His hands gripped her, his fingers biting into the soft flesh of her buttocks as he dragged her through the water and into his own body.

The feel of him against her skin to skin turned her belly soft with hot desire. Impetuously she moved her hips against him, reaching up to wrap her arms around his neck and pull his mouth down towards her own.

She knew that she ought to be shocked by the brazenness of her own behaviour, but instead something inside her was urging her on,

Leon's mouth was on hers and no way was the kiss he was giving her reinforcing the verbal protests and denials he had given earlier.

He was kissing her with a hot passion that more than matched her own, his hands rhythmically kneading her buttocks as he did so.

She could feel him against her, excitingly hard, as his erection rubbed stiffly against her belly. Even the movement of the water seemed to echo the rhythmic thrusts of their bodies as her hips responded to the pressure of his hands, pulling them together.

The reflection of the stars and moon danced on the rocking water. Helplessly Sadie closed her eyes to its mesmerising glitter, only to be subjected to the even more mesmeric effect of Leon's kiss.

She could feel her whole body responding to its passionate demand as she arched up on her toes and pressed herself into him. Her bare breasts were rubbing against his chest, her nipples so aroused by their contact with his body that fierce spirals of sensation coiled from them to flicker like lightning through her.

Their bodies were slickly wet from the pool water, but the heat inside her was generating another kind of wetness within the swelling lips that protected her sex. And not just a wetness, but an ache. Such an ache that she found herself wrapping her arms even more tightly around Leon's neck as she ground her hips into him in open female demand. Her body ached—hurt even—with her need for him.

'You want me here…now?' she could hear Leon demanding thickly as he wrenched his mouth from hers.

Deprived of contact with his mouth, Sadie began to kiss and lick her way along his throat, savouring every taste of him. When she reached his jaw she ran her fingertips experimentally over the shaved line of his beard, exhilarated by the sensually rough feel of him.

His sex, when she touched it, would feel just the opposite—smooth and sleek, the skin tight where it strained over his erection.

Her whole body began to burn and shake, and she made a small, very female growl low in her throat as she nipped urgently at Leon's ear.

Did he really need to hear her say the words? Couldn't he see? Couldn't he feel what was happening to her?

She slid her hands into his hair and tugged it until he once more bent his head towards her.

Against his lips she told him fiercely, 'Yes. I want you. Yes, here—and yes, now!'

She punctuated each word with a kiss, gasping as Leon cut off her breath with her last word, taking her mouth with a savage primitive hunger that sent her blood roaring through her veins and made her weak with reciprocal longing.

His hands were touching her everywhere. Stroking her shoulders, her arms, cupping her breasts and then kneading them with loving attention until she was shuddering pre-orgasmically with hot rivulets of pleasure.

The feel of the pads of his thumbs against her nipples made her cry out—a low, guttural sound that had his hands slipping down, one to grasp the side of her waist, the other stroking over her stomach and then lower, parting the swollen lips of her sex and stroking against her wet eagerness.

At no time in her life had there ever been anything like this! There never had been and never would be again, Sadie acknowledged dizzily as her body responded to Leon's sensual stroking touch with violent, almost climactic little shudders of pleasure.

Instinctively she reached for him, clasping him in her hand, her eyes widening in shock as she realised that she could not fully encompass him.

He felt hot and hard, his sex swollen. Shockingly, she had a sudden savage, surging ache of need to have the feel of him against her lips, to caress and explore him, slowly and thoroughly, but she knew her own body wasn't going to wait for much longer.

As though she had verbalised her urgency and need to him, Leon suddenly grasped her by the waist and lifted her against him.

Eagerly Sadie opened her legs and wrapped them around him, gasping with pleasure as she felt the first thrust of him within her, urging him to move faster and deeper as she clung to him, offering the full pleasure of her body.

The water around them was pounding against the side of the pool in increasingly fast waves, but Sadie wasn't aware of the movement of the water, only the rhythm of their bodies as they rocked together in frantic, desperate need. She could feel the tight circling of her orgasm beginning, her stomach and her thighs tensing as she reached for it, crying out her pleas and praise to Leon.

She could see the rictus mask of his face above her as he drove harder and deeper into her eager flesh. Voluptuously it tightened around him, increasing the intensity of their pleasure.

'Yes…*Yes*!' she moaned. 'Yes. Just like that, Leon… just like that… Mmm…yes. Just—'

The broken sob of her voice was suspended as her whole body tensed and then exploded in a fierce succession of rhythmic contractions.

She could feel the hot surge of Leon's own release pulsing into the warm darkness of her body.

Release, bliss…peace…

She could feel how much she was shaking as she clung to Leon, knowing she was not actually capable of standing on her own two feet.

She felt his lips brush against the dampness of her face.

'Tears?' he whispered. 'I hope they are tears of pleasure?'

'Do you need to ask?' Sadie challenged huskily.

He lifted her out of the water and put her on the side of the pool. Still trembling in the aftermath of her orgasm, she watched as he hauled himself out.

'Stay there,' he ordered her gently.

Dreamily she watched as he went and picked up her discarded robe, returning with it and wrapping her in it.

'Time for bed,' he told her softly, and then he swung her up into his arms and carried her inside.

CHAPTER EIGHT

'BUT this is your bedroom,' Sadie whispered, after he had pushed open the door and carried her over to the bed.

'So it is!' Leon agreed softly. 'Where else did you think you were going to spend the night? Unless, of course, you'd prefer to sleep alone?'

Bravely Sadie met the look he was giving her head-on. No way was she going to pretend that what had just happened between them meant nothing to her, had simply been a mere sexual indulgence.

'I want to sleep with you,' she told him huskily.

'And I certainly want to sleep with you,' Leon told her back, only just managing to restrain himself from adding *for the rest of my life.*

He hadn't been able to believe what was happening when she had come to him in the pool. Just thinking about it now made his body start to harden again.

'I need a shower,' Sadie whispered. 'The pool water...'

'I need one too,' Leon replied, giving her a smokily sensual look as he leaned down towards her and grasped her hand, pulling her gently to her feet and informing her, 'The bathroom's this way, and the shower is plenty big enough for two.'

Sadie knew that he had felt the small quiver of excitement that ran through her body because he turned to look at her, his gaze fastening on her mouth and then dropping very deliberately to her breasts, where her nipples were flaunting their arousal.

He was right about the shower, she noted as she

stepped into the bathroom. The owners of the *mas* had obviously spared no expense in equipping this room. It was larger than her own, with a separate wet area which housed a purpose-built shower.

The water in the pool had left her skin feeling slightly tight and dry, and it was bliss to step into the shower and feel the body-height jets pumping warm, clean water against her skin.

'Want me to do your back for you?'

There was a look in Leon's eyes that made her whole body tingle with excitement. The shower was designed so that it was perfectly possible to wash one's own back, but Sadie had no intention of pointing this fact out to Leon…

She nodded her head and turned her back to him.

The silky-soft feel of the expensive body mousse Leon was massaging into her skin made her sigh in appreciative pleasure. The resultant foam slipped down her legs and floated on the tiles. His hands were moving lower now…beyond her waist. Sadie held her breath and closed her eyes. Her whole body was quivering with expectation and longing. Now that it knew the pleasure Leon would give it, it wanted him all the more.

His fingertips brushed the front of her thigh, and the soft quiver became an involuntary and uncontrollable convulsive shudder. She could feel Leon's lips nuzzling the back of her neck, just below her ear. His hands moved with aching slowness up over the front of her body towards her breasts.

With a small moan Sadie pressed back against him.

'What is it?' he murmured against the ear. 'Do you want me to stop?'

His hands were doing incredible things to her breasts, making her ache for the feel of his mouth against her tight, eager nipples. But Leon did not seem to share her own surging urgency. Instead he continued to stroke and caress her, nibbling little kisses against her neck, sliding his hands over her soap-slicked body. His touch was arousing her to such a frantic pitch that she moaned sharply in frustration and opened her legs, mentally begging him to touch her intimately.

'What is it?' he asked again softly, when her ecstatic writhings wouldn't be stilled. 'What do you want?'

'You know,' Sadie moaned, desperate to grab hold of his hand and place it against her body, but unable to do so because of the way he was still stroking her.

'Tell me,' Leon urged huskily. 'Tell me what you want me to do, Sadie. Show me how you want me to touch you…how you want me to love you… Is it this you want?' he asked warmly as his hand caressed the curve of her hip and slid down over her belly before cupping her sex.

Sadie gasped as she felt the impatient swell of her body, too wrought up to be able to tell Leon what was happening to her. But somehow he knew, she realised, because he turned her round and stared down into her wild open eyes as his fingers answered the urgent need of her body and the fierce, tight explosion of her orgasm brought her into trembling release.

Sadie was awake, but she did not want to open her eyes just in case it had all been only a dream and Leon wasn't actually in bed beside her after all. She knew it must be morning, even with her eyes closed. Somehow she could feel the brightness of the day through her eyelids. If Leon wasn't there…

Cautiously she moved her body, still heavy and soft with satisfaction and love.

Love! Her heart turned over inside her chest. She loved Leon so much... Just the thought of him was enough to—

She stiffened abruptly as the restless movements of her body brought her into contact with warm male flesh. It had happened! She hadn't just imagined it! Leon was here!

Bubbles of joy and excitement fizzed through her blood. With her eyes still closed Sadie nestled closer to him, fitting her body into the curve of his. She could smell the warm, musky scent of him—and it was more aphrodisiacal than any man-made perfume. The soft hair on his chest was tickling her nose. Tenderly she rubbed her lips against his skin, delighting in the secret stolen pleasure of being able to do so whilst he was still asleep. Smiling to herself, she stroked her fingertip lazily along his arm, so different from her own, all powerful muscles and sinews.

Against her body she could feel his stirring. A female shiver of pleasure slowly caressed her own body.

Snuggling further down his body, she teased her tongue-tip around his navel, her hand reaching out to touch and then hold him. It was an extraordinarily sensual and tender thing to feel him growing within her hold, at once both vulnerable and powerful.

Experimentally she started to caress him, enjoying his body's response to her and rewarding it with a soft kiss.

This was an intimacy she hadn't imagined she would ever want to experience, but suddenly she knew just how much she did. The brief touch of her lips became a more intimate and sensual exploration.

'Enjoying yourself?'

The low, groaned words shocked through her. Lifting her head, she turned to look up at Leon. She had been so lost in the enjoyment of what she was doing that she hadn't even realised he was awake.

'I…'

'I certainly was,' he told her thickly, his voice soft with pleasure, 'so don't let me stop you…'

'What time will they be bringing the replacement hire car?' Sadie asked Leon drowsily as she responded to the slow drift of his hands on her body.

They had made love, and then slept, and now Leon was caressing her again.

'Soon,' he told her wryly, removing his hand with obvious reluctance. 'I suppose we'd better make a move.'

There was a note in his voice that made Sadie look enquiringly at him.

'I swore that there was no way I was going to let this happen,' he told her ruefully.

'But you wanted it to?' Sadie questioned him.

'Do you really need to ask?' Leon responded, his voice wry with self-mockery.

Leon's mobile rang as he walked into his hotel room several hours later. He'd just left Sadie at her own room.

'Brad.' He smiled as he recognised the voice of his godfather, the company's and his own solicitor. 'I was going to ring you later, to give you an update on what's happening with the Francine acquisition. Yes, I know things are taking longer than we originally expected,' Leon agreed, still smiling. 'There's been a bit of a complication with the junior shareholder, made more difficult by the fact that she almost backed out of the deal.'

Briefly Leon explained to his godfather exactly what had happened. His smile turned to a frown as he heard Brad asking worriedly, 'What do you mean? We aren't talking about the woman we saw at the trade fair, are we, Leon? Because she looked to me...' He took a pause, and then went on even more worriedly, 'Your father almost lost the business and the shirt off his back, thanks to a conniving, lying woman, Leon, and by the sounds of it you're in danger of having the same thing happen to you!'

'Brad, Sadie isn't like that,' Leon stopped him curtly.

'How can you know that, Leon? You've already said that she's causing problems.'

'Brad, Sadie is not another Miranda.'

'You can't be sure of that, Leon. You're carrying a mighty heavy responsibility on your shoulders—we both know that! Hell, you're a man, Leon, and only human. I understand that. But if you're wrong, you don't need me to tell you how much damage that could do to the business.'

'You worry too much, Brad,' Leon told his godfather affectionately before ending the call, but his frown deepened as he walked over to the window. No matter what his personal feelings for Sadie were, he could not afford to do anything that might put the business at risk.

Sadie was not another Miranda Stanton. He was sure of it. But what if he was wrong? Whatever risks he was prepared to take with his own emotions, he was not prepared to take any with the financial security of the business.

Miranda Stanton!

He had been fourteen, and still mourning his grandmother, when to everyone's shock his father's business partner had died of a heart attack.

Andy and his father had been at school together, and even though the business had originally been Leon's father's idea, he had generously offered Andy a share in it.

They had started out with nothing, but by the time Leon was thirteen the business was beginning to do very well.

And then Andy had got married—to a much younger woman—who none of them had liked.

'If a woman has gold-digger written all over her then that woman is Miranda!' Leon could remember his mother sighing.

Leon could also remember his father coming home one night and telling his mother that he had to go and see the bank. Andy was in a bit of a financial mess, due to Miranda's insistence on an expensive lifestyle, and had asked Leon's father to buy him out of their business.

Generously, because of Andy's desperation, Leon's father had given him the money before the legal documents confirming the buy-out had been signed. A week later, whilst on holiday with Miranda, Andy had had a heart attack and died. And a week after that Miranda had informed Leon's father that she wanted and intended to have the full cash value of Andy's half-share in the business.

It had been useless for Leon's father to protest that Andy had already had the money, and she had known about it. She had pointed out that Leon's father had no legal documentation to prove it.

Leon's father had not given up easily. The matter had even gone to court. But of course legally there had been no proof.

In order to buy her out and meet his legal costs Leon's father had had to mortgage the business up to the hilt, and sell the family home. The family had gone from living in comfort to living from hand to mouth. His parents' smiling faces had become pinched and strained.

Leon had hated Miranda for what she had done to his family. He had vowed then and there that what had happened to his father would never happen to him! And now here was Brad, suggesting that Sadie was potentially another Miranda!

It wasn't true, of course, Leon assured himself. That stubbornness she displayed was defensive rather than manipulative. But a cautionary inner voice reminded him sharply that she had hinted to him about wanting the Grasse property. And there had been all that fuss she had made, both about the Myrrh formula and the creation of a new scent. He had believed her motives to be genuine, if somewhat idealistic and simplistic, but if he was wrong…

It was hardly unknown for an acquisitive woman to use sex to get what she wanted.

Sadie wasn't like that, though!

His intimacy with her was interfering with his analytical abilities as well as potentially threatening to screw up the deal and his life, Leon admitted grimly.

'Face it,' he told himself brutally. 'You've got yourself in way too deep.'

Way, way too deep, he realised.

The best thing he could do right now, he conceded reluctantly, in fact the only thing he could do right now, was to back off and put some space between himself and Sadie.

When the deal had gone through tomorrow, once he had Francine and the Myrrh formula and had fulfilled his duty to the business, then things would be different.

On their way back from the *mas*, he and Sadie had talked briefly about the takeover.

'The legal side of things is pretty well sorted out,' Leon had explained. 'You, Raoul and I sign the papers tomorrow, but first I've told my people to organise an immediate press conference to announce the takeover. It will put an end to all the speculation and gossip that's been going on. I want you to be there, of course, as you're a big part of what will be happening. I'll be making an announcement to the effect that you're going to be working on a new scent under the Francine name, and that we are going to reintroduce a modern version of Mrryh. Unfortunately, virtually as soon as that the press conference is over, I'm going to have to fly back to Australia, via Italy. I've got to see the new designer we're taking on to head the fashion division.'

Leon had felt the beginnings of a sharp ache at the thought of leaving her, but now, he told himself, he was relieved.

Back in her hotel room, Sadie waited, hoping that Leon would ring. He had told her on the way back that he had business matters to attend to, and she understood that, of course, but surely in view of the intimacy they had shared he would also want to be with her as much as possible, before they had to go their separate ways?

Impulsively Sadie went to her door and opened it.

Leon frowned as he opened his door to Sadie's knock.

Smiling tenderly at him, Sadie told him, 'I know you said you had business to attend to, but I thought I could at least be with you—and then, perhaps…'

Her voice trailed away as she saw the way Leon was frowning.

'Leon?' she began uncertainly.

What had happened to the passionate, sensual man she had known so intimately at the *mas*? She could not see anything of him here, in the grim rejection of Leon's reaction to her now.

Anxious and bewildered, Sadie struggled to understand what was happening.

'If it's a bad time…'

Helplessly she looked at him, unable to hide what she was feeling.

As he saw the look in Sadie's eyes Leon's first instinct was to go to her and take her in his arms, but somehow he managed to suppress it. Brad's warning had resurrected some very painful memories. Sadie might not be Miranda, but there were some very complicated issues between them, and there was no way he could allow his own emotions to rule his head now.

'I've got a lot of work to catch up on, Sadie,' he informed her curtly, turning his back on her as he spoke so that he couldn't look into her eyes and be tempted beyond his own self-control.

Reminding himself of his responsibilities to the business, he took a deep breath.

'What happened between us at the *mas*…' he began.

Sadie could not let him go on. Ice-cold anguish and pain were seeping agonisingly through her whole body, filling her with a mixture of anger and disbelief. Only the knowledge that if she remained in Leon's room she would be brutally humiliated made her stop him with a cold stare.

'You don't need to say any more, Leon. I understand perfectly what you mean.'

Not trusting herself to say any more, she whirled round and left.

She felt hot, cold and sick with the pain of being rejected. Burning with anger, she felt torn between two totally conflicting sets of emotions—hating Leon and yet at the same time fully aware of just how much she actually loved him.

Grimly, Leon stared at the empty space where Sadie had been standing. He told himself that he was glad she had left. If she hadn't... Helplessly he moved towards where she had been standing, treacherously allowing himself to breathe in the air still scented by her presence.

She was a passionately and infuriatingly stubborn woman who had the potential to make his life one hell of a lot more complicated than he wanted it to be! And also a lot more pleasurable. It would certainly be more filled with love, with all the things he had denied himself during the years he had focused on building up the business and securing what had been so nearly lost to his family.

Leon's expression became even more grim. He just did not have time for this now. He had to secure Francine— if he didn't, his board would have his guts for breakfast. If he gave in and allowed his feelings for Sadie to take him over and rule his life, how the hell was he going to be able to concentrate wholly on the business? And if he didn't...

Somewhere deep inside him a small, unfamiliar voice asked if he really wanted to devote the rest of his life to the conglomerate...if he wouldn't really rather build a loving relationship than a fat balance sheet. But Leon refused to listen to it.

Sadie stared unseeingly around her room. Leon had rejected her! Her face burned fiercely at the recollection of just how determined and obvious that rejection had been! He had used her and then dropped her, she stormed in furious inward anger, but somehow a part of her recognised that that did not ring true. If Leon had simply wanted a brief sexual fling he could have found someone much more up for that sort of thing than her.

So why had he cast her aside, then, if it wasn't because of that? she demanded of herself, lashing her anger with the whip of her own self-contempt and misery. Why was she trying to find excuses for him? He couldn't have made it plainer that he didn't want her. Sadie felt even more humiliated as she relived his reaction to her uninvited arrival at his room.

Painful as the experiment had been, she discovered that a treacherous part of her had recorded every minute detail about him with a lover's intensity—even small things, like the movement of his hands as he had backed away from her. Were those really the same hands that had drawn her so close, held her so tenderly and touched her so intimately? The harshness of his voice—the same voice which had whispered smokily to her of desire and longing, the same voice which had rung out into the night at the height of passion…. Sadie shivered as she remembered the way his gaze had hardened over her, that same gaze which so very recently had melted and then burned with heat and longing…

What had happened? Why had he changed so abruptly? Instinctively Sadie knew that there was no point in her trying to ask him. His body language had told her exactly how he wanted things to be between them—with as much distance as possible!

Her own pride flared into bitter life. Very well! If that was what he wanted, then that was what he was going to get.

Her emotions were in total confusion, Sadie recognised achingly. She had believed they were falling in love with one another, but now Leon was telling her that he just didn't want to know, that he had changed his mind and that he did not want to build a relationship with her after all.

And, what was more, in telling her that he had also implied that he still expected them to share a business relationship!

One part of her—the part of her which had given him her love and her trust and had had that love rejected—was demanding that she protect herself by having nothing more to do with Leon—ever! But Sadie prided herself on her professionalism, and in her opinion it would just not be morally acceptable for her to back out of the contract negotiations now, just because Leon had rejected her emotionally.

She was in between the proverbial rock and hard place, and her poor heart was being badly hurt by them both!

Perhaps once the contracts had been signed and she became involved in her new role she would be too busy to worry about Leon. Too involved in the excitement of what she was doing to have any time to spare to think about him and how much he had hurt her. In fact, there was no 'perhaps' about it, Sadie decided firmly. That was the way things were going to be! There was no way was she going to languish around nursing a broken heart!

CHAPTER NINE

SHE was, Sadie knew, a little bit late and an awful lot on edge for this morning's press conference—and both her lateness and her edginess were down to one person and one alone. Leon himself!

She was late because if it hadn't been for the fact that she had to be here nothing would have dragged her anywhere she might have to see him. It had taken a hard-fought internal battle to enable herself to put her personal feelings to one side. And, having done so, she was on edge—just in case when she did see him the love she knew full well she still felt for him overwhelmed her and led her into subjecting herself to even more humiliation.

One of the small army of PR people Leon had obviously hired spotted her and bustled purposefully towards her.

'Yes, I'm Sadie,' she admitted, on being questioned. 'Is my cousin Raoul here yet?'

'Yes, I believe he is. If you will come with me, please?'

The press conference that Leon's publicity people had organised was turning out to be a far larger affair than Sadie had expected, and was being held at the house in Grasse—which would still go into Leon's possession with the signing of legal documents later on in the day.

Now, as she looked round the main salon of the house and out into the courtyard, Sadie could only be unwillingly impressed by the transformation Leon's people had managed to achieve in such a short space of time.

Granted, the massed displays of freshly cut flowers helped to draw the eye away from the house's shabbiness, but it had been a master stroke to have some of the old advertisements for Francine perfumes framed and hung on the walls.

Still following the PR girl, Sadie froze suddenly as she looked towards the small stage that had been erected at one end of the room and saw Leon.

The first thing she had done after Leon's rejection of her had been to book herself into a different hotel. She'd chosen a small *pension* in Grasse itself, so that she would not have to run the risk of coming into contact with him. However, she was now discovering that the sight of him after several hours of not seeing him was having much the same effect as the sight of water was likely to have on a man lost in the desert!

He was standing with his back to her, and despite the anger she could still feel burning inside her, her gaze homed in on him like a missile, greedily gathering up every bit of information it could to stockpile inside her heart for the Leon-empty days that lay ahead!

She, who had always always been able to see another person's point of view, was so angry and hurt that she could not extend that generosity to Leon. She felt as though she hated him, but she knew that she loved him! And because of that she pitied herself.

From his position on the small stage—a position he assured himself he had not chosen simply because it gave him an uninterrupted view of anyone entering the room— Leon had witnessed Sadie's arrival, and the manner in which she was so obviously ignoring him. His mouth compressed. He had virtually lost a full nights' sleep— and not because his second in command on the board had telephoned to warn him that another board member, who had been the most keenly opposed to the acquisition of Francine had been demanding to know what was causing the delay, and prophesying that Leon had made a dangerous error in judgement.

No, it wasn't Kevin Linton's fierce antagonism or questioning of his business acumen and judgement that had kept Leon awake last night. Sadie was solely responsible for that! And right now he was sorely tempted to go over to her and remind her in whatever way it took—and so far as he was concerned the more physically intimate the better—of just why she should not ignore him! He ached so badly for her that right now...

Leon's jaw tightened even further. Up until now nothing, no one had had the power to come between him and his dedication to the business. And for it to be Sadie, a woman his solicitor had already cautioned him against...

But Brad didn't know Sadie as he knew her, and Leon swore he never would! No other man ever would, if Leon had his way. No other man would be allowed to so much as look at her, never mind—

Abruptly Leon recognised that he was out of control, that his emotions were careering wildly down a one-way street and that if he didn't get a hold of them...

Out of the corner of his eye he saw a man approaching Sadie, smiling at her, reaching out his hand to touch her... A red mist exploded inside Leon's head. His heart was thumping, adrenalin flooding his body. He wanted—

At Leon's side, the head of the PR company interrupted his dangerous flow of thoughts.

'I think everyone is here. We should begin the conference, I think. The press are beginning to grow impatient...'

At the same moment, this mystery man was raising

Sadie's hand to his lips. The PR executive frowned in confusion as she heard Leon give a low, muted growl of male anger.

'Merci, Monsieur Fontaine,' Sadie said politely, thanking the man who had been praising the scent she was wearing. Still smiling, she firmly extracted her hand from his grasp.

'Come on, Sadie. Leon wants us both up on the stage,' Raoul announced, suddenly appearing at her side and taking hold of her arm.

Sadie could feel the PR executive and Leon looking at them as she and Raoul approached the stage. Immediately she averted her face, looking very deliberately past Leon, her chin lifting with haughty female pride.

Out of the corner of her eye she caught a glimpse of the icy, brief look Leon gave her. From out of nowhere, Sadie jealously wondered, would the elegant Frenchwoman at his side be the one to share his bed tonight?

The pain that tore at her almost made her cry out loud!

Unable to stop herself, she watched as Leon strode to the front of the stage and picked up the microphone.

'I hope this is going to be quick,' Raoul muttered at her side. 'The sooner Leon's cheque is in my pocket the happier I shall be! I must say you don't look very happy for someone who's about to pocket a couple of million euros!'

'Francine means far more to me than money, Raoul,' Sadie reminded her cousin in a determined whisper. 'You know that. If it wasn't—'

A fierce 'shush' from one of the hovering PR personnel made Sadie go red and stop speaking, to concentrate instead on what Leon was saying to the assembled press.

Determinedly Sadie tried not to be aware of him, not to think about him, not to remember. But as fierce as her anger was, her love was even fiercer, and helplessly she turned her head to look longingly towards him, taking advantage of his audience's concentration on what he was saying to gaze hungrily at his dark-suited back view.

Just watching him made her whole body quiver with aching need.

Leon had reached the end of his short speech confirming the takeover.

Someone from the floor called up.

'Are you intending to keep the Francine name?'

'Of course,' Leon responded immediately.

'And the Francine perfumes?' someone else challenged him, 'What about them?

'So far as I am concerned there is only one Francine perfume,' Leon responded coolly, 'and that is Myrrh. I am delighted to be able to tell you that the great-great-great-granddaughter of the founder of the house is going to be working for us—not only on adapting the Myrrh formula to suit modern-day tastes, but also on creating a new perfume under the Francine name. As you will all know, Sadie Roberts is already well regarded in the business as a gifted creator of exclusive scents, and I am delighted to be able to introduce her to you as Francine's new creative director.'

As Leon turned to look at her, Sadie stood up on cue and walked towards him, knowing that he intended to introduce her to the audience.

He had extended his hand towards her in what appeared to be a gesture of warmth and appreciation, but Sadie deliberately stopped just short of it—and him—and for her pains received a look from him that threatened to collapse her fragile pride into dust.

Turning his head so that no one else could hear him, he said softly, 'This is a business arena we are in today, Sadie, not a personal one.'

Equally softly, Sadie hissed back, 'There is no personal arena for us any more, Leon.'

Whilst their gazes were still locked in silent combat, one of the reporters in the audience called, 'As you say, we know of Mademoiselle Sadie, but surely it is true that she only creates perfumes made from natural sources? Are we to understand that from now on Francine perfumes are to be created in the same way?'

Sadie took a deep breath, wholly professional now as she waited confidently for her moment to make public the compromise she and Leon had reached—publicly for Francine, but privately in her heart for her grandmother. But before she could say anything Leon had reached for the microphone.

'No, the new Francine perfumes will be scents that will be affordable for every woman who wishes to wear them, and for that reason they will—in common with most modern perfume houses—be created without the need for expensive and sometimes unreliable raw materials.'

Rigid with disbelief, Sadie drew in her breath, the audience momentarily forgotten as she turned to Leon and burst out, white-faced with fury, 'How can you say that? You know I would *never* agree to work wholly with synthetics!'

The press conference was over, the eagerly curious audience having been hurriedly despatched by the PR company, and Sadie and Leon were confronting one another across the upstairs room of the house where they had first officially met.

'How could you do that?' Sadie demanded bitterly,

swinging round from where she had been looking out of the window to face Leon. 'How could you lie like that?'

'Lie?' Leon stopped her, his voice ominously quiet. 'I haven't lied, Sadie. You assured Raoul that you were in agreement with my plans. You accepted both that the Myrrh perfume rightly belongs to Francine and that you were willing to work on revamping its formula and creating a new perfume using man-made materials.'

Sadie had never looked more beautiful or more desirable to him than she did right now, Leon acknowledged, and he felt the stomach-clenching kick of his own fierce need thrust through his body.

'I assured Raoul of no such thing!' Sadie insisted. She felt almost incandescent with shock and rage, barely able to speak for the ferocity of her fury. She knew she'd been lied to and deceived—and not just by her cousin!

'You must have known that I would never, ever give such an agreement,' she threw at Leon passionately. 'I can't believe you can possibly have thought that I would ever agree to work exclusively with synthetics when you know how important it is to me...'

Leon couldn't believe what he was hearing. This was his worst nightmare scenario come to life! There he was, facing a stubborn, emotional woman who threatened the security of his business.

Just wait until Kevin Linton got to hear about this! He had been opposed to the Francine acquisition right from the start, stating that it simply did not have legs, and now, Leon realised bitterly, his adversary might be right.

'You tricked me,' she told him fiercely.

'I tricked you!' Leon snapped, adding, 'It seems to me that it's very convenient for you that Raoul is nowhere to be found!'

'Convenient for *me*?' Sadie felt as though she might

explode with the ferocity of her rage and sense of ill-usage. 'Raoul assured me that you were willing to compromise, to allow me to create a perfume that was a blend of both naturals and synthetics—a perfume that—'

'What? You expected me to let you create a perfume for selfish women with too much money who don't give a damn about anyone other than themselves? No way. Not now. Not ever!' Leon told her, shaking his head to emphasise his feelings. 'I thought I'd already made it plain to you, Sadie, that I want a perfume that all women can enjoy.'

'All women?' Sadie's lip curled in furious contempt. 'You don't give a damn about my sex, Leon. All you care about is making money—well rest assured you aren't going to make any from me, or from the Myrrh formula!'

Leon had had enough! Before he could stop himself he was reaching for Sadie and wrapping his arms around her, smothering her angry, heated words with the equally heated pressure of his mouth.

For one single heartbeat Sadie tried to resist him, but it was impossible. A hot tide of longing was already surging through her, obliterating her defences as it did so. Helplessly she clung to him, returning his kiss with equal intensity. Their mouths meshed, their bodies defying the pressure of their mutual anger.

'Sadie, you've got to see reason,' Leon growled against her mouth.

'*I've* got to see reason?' Immediately Sadie pulled back from him, her breasts rising and falling with the rapidity of her aroused breathing.

'You verbally agreed to sign our contract, and morally—'

'Morally, nothing,' Sadie declared, incensed, still trying to come down from the emotional impact of his kiss.

Leon froze. Suddenly he was fourteen again, witnessing the argument between his father and Miranda. 'Morally?' She had laughed mockingly. 'Legally, you have
nothing! Now legally *he* had nothing. There was no wit-
ness to her verbal agreement, no contract, no Myrrh and
no Sadie.

Anger, despair and the sharpest pain he had ever
known roiled inside him.

'My God, Brad was right to warn me. You are another
Miranda Stanton,' he burst out, white-faced.

His words barely registered in Sadie's consciousness.
Suddenly she was sick to her stomach as a horrible
thought hit her. Had Leon taken her to bed in a cold-
blooded attempt to soften her up? Had he ultimately intended to persuade her to create a wholly synthetic perfume?

Torn apart by her pain, she told him emptily, 'I will
never, ever create a synthetic perfume, Leon. Never!'

Without waiting for his reply she turned and walked
unsteadily out of the room.

Leon stared after Sadie's departing back and tried to
fight down his own emotions. Suddenly he had the most
intense longing to go after her and stop her—tell her...
Tell her what? That he was afraid he might love her?
Tell her about Miranda Stanton and that he dreaded that
she might be just like her? That he was afraid she might
somehow tempt him into putting his love for her before
his responsibility towards the business? That he was terrified that if he touched her now he would tell her she
could create her damned perfume out of the stars in the
sky and he would drag them down out of it for her if
only she would tell him she loved him back?

Oh, Kevin would love that!

He needed a straitjacket!

He needed...

Leon gave a groan as his memory provided him with a very detailed and illuminating image of just exactly what he *did* need. That was Sadie, soft, warm, naked, willing and loving in his arms—whispering to him, kissing him, holding him, telling him things that would send him plain crazy and then putting those words into actions, sweet, hot, sexy promises of intimate pleasure that...

Leon ground his teeth in savage frustration. Without Sadie and the Myrrh formula Francine was doomed to failure. And if it failed it would cost his group of companies millions of pounds and a public loss of face from which there could be no recovery.

His own position and his own fortune were unassailable, but Leon was all too aware of the vulnerability of those who had invested in his companies and in him. He had a moral obligation to his shareholders that he had to put ahead of his own feelings.

CHAPTER TEN

GRIMLY Leon put down his mobile. He had been trying to get in touch with Raoul for the last four days—ever since he had returned to Sydney, in fact—but there was just no answer either to his calls or his e-mails.

From the modern offices of Stapinopolous Inc. Leon could look down onto the harbour, but the fabulous view before him could not hold his attention today.

'Could I have a word, Leon?'

Blanking his thoughts, Leon shot Kevin Linton an assessing look.

'Not if you want to regurgitate everything we've already discussed, Kev,' he answered calmly.

'Hell, Leon. You're talking to me as though we're on opposite sides of the fence! No one has the interest of this corporation at heart more than me; you know that!'

'I also know, Kev, that so far you've tried to block just about every expansion programme we've adopted, and—'

'Leon, we're an Aussie business and, yeah, I think we should stay that way. All this tomfoolery about buying into stuff in Europe. I just don't get it.'

'We live in a shrinking world, Kev. From a TV programme beamed out across it, viewers can see and want a thousand products—that's a fact I don't need to prove. We're already well-established in the market, but if we are to expand...'

'Leon, I know what you're saying—but to buy a run-down perfume business...' Kevin shook his head. 'It seems to me that you've made a real error or judgement—especially when we take into account the fact that the deal hasn't gone through yet, and all on account of this woman!'

'The deal will go through,' Leon told him tersely. 'And "this woman" as you call her is—' Leon stopped, his heart doing a slow, painful somersault. This woman was *his* woman. And she had got so far inside his head and his heart that he could barely function without her.

'Well, it's your reputation that's lying on the line, Leon, not mine. But I have to tell you there's no way I will agree to being held to ransom and having to pay out good money for something we could damn well hire a chemist to make for us for peanuts.'

Somehow Leon managed to hold on to his temper. He had made it perfectly clear to Kevin why they were buying Francine and right now he was in no mood for Kevin's favourite kind of power-game-playing.

'And this woman—the one who's causing us all this trouble. Honestly, Leon, she sounds like a real bitch from hell.'

'Sadie is no such thing!'

Leon had spoken before he could stop himself, leaping immediately and instinctively to Sadie's defence in a way that shocked him just as much as it had obviously surprised his co-director.

Why was he so bent on defending a woman who had caused him so much trouble? Because he was a fool, that was why! Or because deep down inside himself he knew—just knew—that Sadie was not another Miranda? Not matter how much the facts might suggest that she was.

After Kevin had gone Leon wondered broodingly what he was doing, spending so much time thinking about

Sadie over there in Europe, when there was so much that was surely more important that needed his attention right here in Sydney.

The truth was, though, that he just could not get her out of his head. Instead of thinking about his upcoming meeting with Mario Testare, the designer he had head-hunted to take charge of the ageing fashion house he had taken over five years ago, and the meeting he had planned with CEO of the luxury leather goods arm of the business, all he could think about was Sadie, he acknowledged angrily.

There hadn't been a single second in his life when Leon had envisaged himself in this kind of situation. Marriage, children—yes, he wanted both—one day. He was part Greek, after all. But falling in love, and the intensity of emotion Sadie aroused in him—these were just not part of his game plan at all.

Sadie! Hell, he was thinking about her again! Only because of his concern over the problems she had caused by refusing to sign the contract, Leon assured himself firmly.

But it wasn't just her signature on that contract he needed. What he also needed was her mouth on his, her body in his arms, her soft, sexy voice whispering those things in his ear that made him just ache to—

Stop that, he warned himself sternly. What he absolutely *had* to have was her agreement to creating a new perfume. A saleable, affordable perfume. And that perfume had to be made from synthetics. Didn't it? Though in the heat of their argument Sadie had implied that she was prepared to compromise, and to work on creating a blended scent.

Yes, and it would be a blended scent with so many

expensive ingredients that it would be far too expensive for any mass market, Leon told himself firmly.

But what if there were some way such a perfume could be created at an affordable cost? What if he could find a way to prove that to himself and to his board? Maybe then…

Why was he was wasting time he didn't have allowing his thoughts to dwell on the most aggravating and impossible woman God had ever created?

He picked up his mobile. He suspected that Raoul was not taking his calls because he was afraid Leon would call in the advance he had given him against the acquisition. Leon knew that he had to take on Francine now, thanks to Kevin, or face the possibility of a vote of no confidence from his own board. And to that end he needed to speak with Raoul. And with Sadie!

Frowning, he put down his mobile. If Raoul would not answer his calls then there was only one thing he could do!

Striding across his office, he sat down and buzzed for his secretary.

'Book me a flight to Nice, will you, please?'

'And a hotel?' his secretary asked. 'Do you want to stay in Mougins again, or…?'

Leon hesitated. Mougins. That was where he and Sadie…

Sadie stared in disbelief at the e-mail she had just received. It was a request—no, not a request but a demand, and a very tersely worded one at that—from Leon, insisting that she present herself in Grasse 'in order that a discussion can take place to resolve current difficulties.'

Just knowing that Leon had sent the e-mail was causing her heart to thud and her whole body to react. If a mere e-mail from him could fill her with such a savage mixture of longing pain and anger then what was the reality of him likely to do?

Cravenly, she was tempted to simply ignore the message. But logically she knew that she couldn't.

Whilst she was still staring at the screen her telephone rang.

As she picked up the receiver she heard Raoul's voice exclaiming urgently, 'Sadie! I need to talk to you!'

'I've got Leon's e-mail, Raoul, and if you're phoning to try and persuade me to talk with him—' Sadie began.

But Raoul cut across her, announcing grimly, 'Sadie, you've got to help me. If you don't Leon could take me to court and claim back the money he's advanced me against the acquisition of Francine—and if he does that I'm in real trouble.'

So, Raoul had lied to her and about her, Sadie told herself. But he was still her cousin, and oddly it was easier to forgive him than it was for her to forgive Leon. Because Leon had hurt her so much more? Or because she loved Leon so much more?

Just don't go there, she advised herself.

'Raoul, nothing's changed,' she warned her cousin. 'I will not allow Leon to have the Myrrh formula, and neither will I create a synthetic perfume for him.'

'Sadie, all he wants to discuss is the acquisition of Francine,' Raoul reassured her. 'Nothing more than that. And if you don't agree to sell to him, Sadie, I'm going to be in one hell of a mess.'

'If you're lying to me again, Raoul—' Sadie began, but she knew that she was weakening and she suspected that Raoul knew it too.

By the time she had replaced the receiver she had agreed to go back to France.

*   *   *

'What's wrong?' Mary asked Sadie sympathetically, whilst her teenage niece Caroline, who was visiting her, gleefully explored Sadie's workroom. 'Still brooding about Leon? You haven't been able to put what happened with him behind you, have you? Despite what you said to me!'

Sadie had, of course, told Mary everything that had happened in France with Leon. Well, almost everything! She had been so upset on her return to Pembroke that she had not been able to stop herself from pouring her heart out to her. Then, she had claimed that she was going to make herself believe that she hadn't even met Leon, never mind fallen so deeply in love with him! But, as Mary had just pointed out, forgetting Leon had proved to be impossible!

'It doesn't matter how I feel, Mary. I told you what he said to me, how all he wants is for me to create a synthetic scent for him. I shall never do that! Never!' she announced doggedly.
'I've agreed to go to France to see him, but that's for Raoul's sake. If Leon thinks he can make me change my mind…'

Mary gave her a shrewd look.

'Please don't take this the wrong way, Sadie. You're my friend, and the last thing I want to do is to hurt or offend you, but it seems to me from all that you have said about Leon that the two of you are perfectly matched and both as stubborn as one another!' she said gently.

Whilst Sadie glowered, unwilling to accept her friend's assessment, Mary went on ruefully. 'Love on its own isn't enough, you know.' She insisted semi-severely. 'There has to be a willingness to understand and accept one's other half's point of view. Haven't either of you heard of the word "compromise"?'

Before Sadie could answer, Caroline came out of the workroom to join them.

'Sadie, that perfume you're wearing is delicious,' she began longingly. 'Isn't there any way you could create something similar but not quite as expensive?' she asked plaintively. 'Something that a poor student like me could afford?'

After Mary and Caroline had gone Sadie went into her workroom. Caroline's comments about her perfume had struck home and made her feel a little bit guilty. Of course it was only natural that any woman would want to be able to wear a 'good' scent, but Caroline's innocent question had forced Sadie to reassess her own stance and ask herself if there really was a way man-made scents could be blended to create a good perfume that would be within the means of all women.

It wasn't because she wanted to give in to Leon that she was thinking like this, trying to find a way to make an expensive traditional perfume more financially accessible, Sadie assured herself. It was just that the look of longing in Caroline's eyes had made her see things differently. It would certainly be a challenge for her!

But nowhere near as much of a challenge as winning Leon's love!

Angry with herself, Sadie paced her workroom floor. What kind of woman was she to want to win the love of a man who had so humiliatingly rejected her?

She tried to make herself focus on her work, but all she could think of was Leon and that final destructive scene between them.

Had he any idea just how much he had shocked and hurt her? Accusing her of...

Sadie frowned, suddenly remembering just what he had said to her. *'You are another Miranda Stanton.'*

Who was Miranda Stanton? And what did she have to do with Leon's rejection of her?

Sadie stared at her computer and then quickly began to type, her fingers trembling slightly.

By the time Sadie had finished re-reading the information her computer search had brought up for the third time she was having to swallow hard to suppress her tears of compassion.

The story of what had happened had been laid bare for her through newspaper archive accounts, but reading it had not shocked her as much as the one photograph she had seen of a fourteen-year-old Leon, so tall that he had been almost shoulder to shoulder with his father, his gaze fixed on his father's face.

What a dreadful time that must have been for the whole family; what a dreadful thing Miranda Stanton had done. And what an appalling insult Leon had hurled at her when he had drawn a parallel between this woman and herself! Torn between exasperation, anger and aching love, Sadie didn't know whether to run towards her up-coming meeting in France with Leon, or to run from it!

CHAPTER ELEVEN

THE sun might be shining down warmly, but its heat wasn't enough to melt the ice-cold despair and pain lodged in her heart, Sadie realised sadly as she stepped out of her taxi and looked up at the front of the Mougins hotel, which was where Leon had elected to hold their meeting.

Sadie wished he had chosen anywhere but here—the place where she had begun to love him and where she had believed he had begun to love her in return.

She was early for her meeting with Leon and Raoul, and she was tired—she hadn't been sleeping properly at home, and last night, after her arrival at the small hotel in Cannes where she was staying, every time she had managed to fall asleep she had ended up dreaming about Leon! And what dreams they had been! Her face grew hot at the memory of them. But nowhere near as hot as her body had been last night!

She had nearly half an hour to waste before her meeting, so Sadie thought she might as well wander through the hotel's gardens. But she would not follow the path where Leon had kissed her for the first time!

On the balcony of his suite Leon tensed as he looked out of the window and saw Sadie slowly walking through the garden. He tried to close his mind and his heart to the effect the sight of her was having on him, but it was impossible! His body had already made its feelings perfectly clear.

161

As he watched he saw Sadie turn and start in the opposite direction.

Unable to stop himself, he left his balcony, taking the flight of stone steps that led directly into the gardens two at a time, and calling out her name as he followed her down the path.

The moment she heard Leon calling her name Sadie froze. Somehow she made herself turn round and confront him.

He looked grimly forbidding, and for a moment her own resolve faltered. This was a business meeting—nothing more, she reminded herself. If she had hopes and dreams that were not going to be fulfilled, then she had only herself to blame.

Silently she fell into step beside him, careful to keep a clear distance between their bodies and he escorted her back towards his suite.

'Is Raoul here?' she asked, and then frowned as her mobile rang.

Excusing herself, she fished it out of her bag, her frown deepening when she realised that the caller was Raoul himself.

'Sadie—I just thought I'd let you know that I have decided it's best if you and Leon sort out your differences alone. Leon knows that I am not the one holding up completion of the acquisition. And you know how very important it is to me that this deal goes through. As your cousin, I beg you to remember this and to—'

'Raoul, I am with Leon now,' Sadie interrupted him sharply. 'Where are you? Why aren't you—?'

She gave a small hiss of exasperation as Raoul immediately ended the call.

'That was Raoul,' she told Leon. 'He—'

'I gathered what he said,' Leon informed her curtly.

They had reached the stone staircase now, and Leon stood to one side to allow Sadie to precede him. Warily, she did so.

'Raoul wants me to agree to sell my share of the business to you,' she told Leon. 'I understand that you have advanced certain monies to him and that legally you are entitled to demand their repayment in full.'

'And so, to protect Raoul from such a fate, you are willing to—?'

'I am willing to sell my share of Francine to you, Leon. That is all I offer. Nothing else.'

She had just started to mount the steps but stopped, turning to look at him. He was still a couple of stairs lower, and Sadie suddenly became aware that they were on the same eye level.

Disconcertingly, she realised that Leon's gaze had dropped to her mouth. And that her mouth had suddenly become soft and eager with the memory of his kisses. Sadie could swear she felt her lips warming and parting, almost pouting as they gloried in Leon's visual attention.

And what was sauce for the goose...

Whilst Leon's attention was so engaged there was nothing to stop her from looking at him...at his face, his skin, his own mouth.

She was losing it, and in a big, big way, Sadie recognised helplessly when she heard herself give a small betraying moan as she leaned hungrily towards him.

'Sadie!'

Was that a warning to stay away from him, or a warning that he could not...?

'Sadie?'

'Leon...' Sadie was shocked to discover herself murmuring his name against his jaw, and to note that she was wrapped wonderfully and blissfully tightly in his arms.

She was perfectly sure that if she turned her head, like this...

A shock of savagely hot pleasure burned through her as she returned the fierce passion of Leon's kiss, somehow managing to wriggle her arms free so that she could fling them around him to hold him as tightly as he was holding her.

The unashamed hardness of his arousal against her body reminded her vividly of last night's dreams. But this wasn't a dream. This was wonderfully, gorgeously real!

Behind her closed eyelids, Sadie could see a bed, a large, wonderful bed, in a shadowy private room. And on those bed she could see Leon naked, aroused, reaching for her...

Leon, who had rejected her, who had compared her to a woman he hated...a woman who—

'No!'

Fiercely, Sadie pushed Leon away.

'This isn't why I'm here, Leon,' she told him firmly, quickly turning her head so that he wouldn't have the opportunity to look into her eyes and see just how very vulnerable to him she actually was. After all, she had her pride, didn't she? She wasn't going to give him the opportunity to reject her a second time, was she?

'As I've already said, for Raoul's sake I am prepared to sell my share of Francine to you. So, now you've got what you want, if you don't mind I—'

'Got what I want? And if I haven't got everything I want?' Leon asked softly.

Sadie could feel her heart hammering against her ribcage This wasn't a verbal prelude to a declaration of love or a plea for understanding and forgiveness, she told herself quickly. So there was no point in her stupid heart hoping that it was. Leon just wasn't that kind of man. Leon didn't want her. He wanted...

'I haven't changed my mind about the Myrrh formula, Leon—that formula was entrusted to me by my grandmother. Its history meant a great deal to her. If I were to sell it or change it in any way—' Her mouth twisted with bitter sadness. 'But of course I can hardly expect you to understand how I feel, can I? After all, in your eyes I'm another Miranda Stanton. I knew from your tone of voice that you were insulting me, Leon, but I didn't realise just how much until I read up on just what she had done! I can understand how frightened and vulnerable you must have felt when she—'

'I felt no such thing!'

The harshness in his voice made Sadie turn her head to look at him. It was obvious that she had found a chink in his emotional armour, but that knowledge made her feel more sad than triumphant.

'Have you any idea how I felt, knowing you had compared me to her Leon? A woman so morally deficient, a woman who delighted in hurting others, in cheating them for her own selfish ends?'

Every word Sadie said was making Leon feel increasingly uncomfortable and angry. He had spent the whole of the previous two days talking with one of the French perfume industry's foremost chemists, trying to find out if there was a way that he and Sadie could reach a compromise over the creation of a new scent, so that he could tell her... But clearly all she wanted to do was touch an old but still raw wound he had no wish to have prodded and probed.

'Sadie, I know you're no Miranda. I...' He pushed his hand into his hair and gave a small exasperated shrug.

'Oh, you say that now, Leon, when you want me to

agree to sell my share in Francine,' Sadie told him coldly. 'But there really isn't any need for you to lie to me. I've already told you I—'

'Lie to you! What the hell—! My God, Sadie I'm doing my damnedest to build bridges here, but as fast as I try you go pulling them down.'

'I've had enough of this,' Sadie told him. 'I'm not a complete fool, Leon—no matter what you might think. I can do simple maths and add up two and two, you know. You think that every woman you come across in business is potentially another Miranda, and I can understand why you're afraid of history repeating itself, but—'

'Hell and damn it, Sadie, I am not afraid of anything or anyone,' Leon growled savagely. 'And right now you are seriously off topic.'

'Yes, you are, Leon,' Sadie countered simply. 'You're afraid now and you will continue to be afraid all your life—unless you learn to let go of the past and—'

Sadie gave a small gasp of shock as suddenly she was in Leon's arms and the words she had been about to speak were smothered by the hot pressure of his mouth grinding down fiercely on hers.

She ought to stop him. She knew that. Or at least her head knew it. Her body might know it, but if it did it certainly didn't seem to care, because it was reacting to him with love-crazed enthusiasm: her lips softening and parting, her tongue stroking hungrily against his, her arms lifting to hold him equally as tightly as he was holding her. Her body was pressing itself into him, her hips grinding achingly against the hard thrust of his erection.

The sound of their breathing, the soft little sighs and moans of pleasure Sadie was giving and the thick, raw muffled responses from Leon filled the air around them.

Dizzily Sadie acknowledged that if this was war no way was she going to sue for peace!

When Leon's hand cupped her breast she moaned an appreciative response. When she tugged his shirt free of his jeans and allowed her hands the pleasure of caressing his warm bare skin he returned the compliment by sliding his hand beneath her tee shirt with gratifying impatience and eagerness.

Her nipple pushed eagerly against the thin fabric of her bra, seeking the skin to skin touch of his hand just as eagerly as his erection was demanding hers.

Between hungrily passionate kisses their clothes were quickly and mutually discarded. The desk was behind them and Sadie murmured in approval as Leon made good use of it, by lifting her onto it.

The warm sunlight through the window dusted gold over Leon's warmly tanned skin, finding in the dark shadowing of hair glints of tawny warmth. Sadie clung to him as he reached for her, wrapping herself tightly around him, welcoming each hungry thrust of his body within her own, encouraging his deeper and deeper penetration of her as her need for him rocketed out of control.

They came together quickly and ferociously, the explosion of pleasure inside her leaving Sadie's body trembling.

As the heat left her body and the red burst of need clouding her brain lifted, she wondered bleakly what on earth she had done. But as she made to pull away from Leon he pulled her closer, cradling her against his body.

'No. I want you here with me, Sadie. In my arms. Heaven knows I've dreamed about holding you in them damn near every night since we've been apart.'

Silently Sadie looked at him. Her heart had begun to jump giddily around inside her ribcage, and she wanted to tell it to stop, to realise as she did that Leon was afraid of the commitment it ached for them to share.

'And in my bed!' Leon was continuing, his voice growing thicker with every word. 'Not just now, tonight, but every night, Sadie. You were right when you accused me of being afraid,' he told her abruptly. 'But what I'm most afraid of right now is loving you, Sadie. I want you in my life full-time, with all that entails. You could never be another Miranda. I knew that all along. But to have you back out of the deal I'd spent so much time putting together, knowing how my board were likely to react when some of them had been against the whole thing from the start...'

'What happened to your father must have been hard for you,' Sadie said quietly.

She could see from the look in Leon's eyes that a part of him wanted to back off from this kind of discussion, but to Sadie it was important that they talked about it. '*Very* hard for you,' she added with soft encouragement, waiting, wanting him to open up to her and allow her into his pain.

The look on his face said that she had gone too far, trespassed too far, but Sadie wasn't about to back off!

They had shared one very important kind of intimacy, the kind of intimacy where she had opened herself to him as a woman, and now it was time for him to open himself to her as a man!

'Hard?' His mouth twisted bitterly. 'I was fourteen and my father was my hero. He had worked damn near a ten-hour day seven days a week to get the business off the ground. You should have seen the pride in his face the day he took my mother and me to see the house he had bought for us. That meant so much to him. That he was able to provide for us, to give my mother all the things she'd had to do without whilst he was getting the business up and running. He told me that one day I would take over from him...but not until I'd been to college and seen a bit of the world. He wanted me to have the opportunities he hadn't been able to have himself! And then Andy died, and Miranda...' Leon paused. 'That was hard, seeing my father going virtually overnight from a man of pride and self-respect to someone...'

Unable to stop herself, Sadie reached out and covered Leon's hand with her own in a gesture of womanly comfort and understanding.

'You must have felt very angry, and very afraid.' she said gently. When he looked at her she added, 'You were only a boy, Leon. Fourteen...'

'Fourteen is only four years off manhood,' Leon told her curtly. 'What happened then made me the man I am today, Sadie. A man who always puts the security of the business ahead of everything else in my life.'

He paused to look at her before adding gruffly, 'And then you came along, and suddenly...What was happening between us wasn't in my game plan—and you were a woman I was involved with on a business footing. When I was with you, you blew my ability to rationalise clean out of the water. All I wanted...all I needed was you. Don't you see?' he growled. 'What was happening between us pushed me off base and made me feel...'

'Vulnerable?' she suggested softly.

For a moment she thought he wasn't going to reply.

This man, *her* man, she acknowledged with a tiny shiver of fierce pleasure, was quite definitely one tough alpha male.

'If you want to put it that way,' he agreed, almost grudgingly.

'And that was why you rejected me?'

Sadie didn't wait for his reply; she could see it in his eyes. The best way to teach someone was by example, she reminded herself. And, that being the case, if she wanted Leon to talk to her about his feelings perhaps she would talk about her own first!

Taking a deep breath, she asked him slowly, 'Have you any idea what rejection does to a woman, or at least to this woman, when she's given herself in love to the man she thinks shares her feelings? When she's already planning their future together, even imagining having his babies? Only to be told that she's got it wrong, that he doesn't want her; that he doesn't share her feelings?'

'You were doing that? Imagining having my babies?' His voice was thick with awe, raw with emotion. 'You were imagining...?'

As he took her in his arms, Leon whispered against her mouth, 'We've got to find a way to make this work, Sadie. We will find a way!'

Pushing him away, Sadie warned him, 'I won't change my mind about the Myrrh formula, Leon. Nor about working with synthetics.'

Leon brushed his thumb against Sadie's lips.

'No words now, Sadie. Not when there is so much I want to communicate to you in so many other ways—with my hands, with my mouth, with my body!' he added sensuously as he felt her lips open to caress the hard pad of his thumb.

Tomorrow he would tell her about his meeting with the chemist, and that he planned to put to his board the proposal that they invest in creating a scent which would combine the best of both natural ingredients and synthetic that could be afforded by women all over the world. But right now he had far, far more important things on his mind than mere business!

As her tongue probed the ridges of flesh on Leon's thumb, Sadie opened her arms to him, moaning with pleasure as he bent his head to her breast and started to feather delirium-inducing caresses against its taut peak.

CHAPTER TWELVE

'YES, Raoul. I've told Leon that I'm prepared to sell him my share of Francine,' Sadie confirmed patiently into her mobile.

She was still in Leon's suite at the hotel, having spent the entire night with him, and her body throbbed blissfully with that very special physical ache that comes with sexual fulfilment.

Leon had left half an hour earlier, telling her that he had a meeting to go to but insisting that she was to stay until he returned.

'We have a great deal to talk about,' he had whispered as he kissed her. 'And I do not mean the Francine contract!'

Sadie's mouth curled into a happy smile now as she spoke to her cousin.

'I've also told Leon that I haven't changed my mind about either the Myrrh formula or creating a new synthetic scent for him,' she warned Raoul.

'Well, he won't be bothered about that,' Raoul interrupted her carelessly. 'I've heard that he's already in negotiation with Arnaud Lebrun, and he's supposed to be the best chemist in the whole of the perfume industry. If you want my opinion, you've been a fool to turn down the kind of opportunity Leon would have given you and your career, but it was your choice! Lebrun will give Leon what he wants! But at least you've had the sense to agree to sell your share of Francine to Leon,' Raul continued, oblivious to the deathblow he had dealt her.

Numbly, Sadie ended the call. Logically there was no valid reason why she should feel the way she was right now! Leon had every right to hire someone else to do what she had refused to do. But last night he had told her that they would find a way to work things out, and she had believed that he'd meant he was prepared to compromise, just as she was herself.

But she could not have been more wrong.

Once again pain, anger, desolation and a feeling of betrayal filled her. These were now familiar, destructive and unwanted feelings for Sadie. Feelings she had told herself—and believed—in Leon's arms last night that she would never experience again.

And what made it all so much worse was that Leon hadn't even warned her what he was planning to do. In bed last night he had as good as told her he loved her. But how could he when…?

She was on the point of leaving when Leon walked into the suite.

When she made no move to go to him, and then stepped back out of arm's reach when he came to her, he stood still and frowned.

'What is it? What's wrong?' He asked immediately.

'Was your appointment today with Arnaud Lebrun?' she challenged him.

'Yes, it was. But—'

Sadie felt sick with shock and pain.

'Leon, this just isn't going to work between us!' she told him fiercely.

'Last night I thought that perhaps… That given what I believed we felt for one another we might be able to reach a compromise with regard to Francine's new scent. But though I know that logically I have no right to feel this way because you have approached Lebrun to create

a new perfume for you. I just wish you had told me—
that's all. I had hoped that you were prepared to meet me
halfway. I just wish that you cared enough—not just
about me, but about my professional opinion, my work
ethic—to want to find that compromise, just as I want to
find it with you! But now…'

'Sadie—'

'No. It's no good. Being involved sexually with you
is just not enough for me. And I don't even think that
being involved with you emotionally is either. I'm a modern woman, Leon. I want to play a full role in my partner's life. I want my own career too.'

'Sadie, I went to see Lebrun to ask his advice about
the feasibility of creating a new scent that was a combination of natural materials and synthetics, that was all!
He's the best in the business and I wanted to see not only
if he thought if it could be done but also if it *was* done
if it could be done within a budget that would make it
affordable to every woman who wanted to wear it. I'd
already decided that I was going to strong-arm my board,
even put money in myself, if that was what it took to get
the thing off the ground. And do you know why I was
doing all that, Sadie? Do you know why I've been pacing
my bedroom floor at night and staring out of my damn
office window instead of concentrating on my business?
Do you even care why? Or are you so damned intent on
being right that you just can't see beyond that? I did it
for you…for my love for you and our future together. It
was for *you*, Sadie!'

As she stared at him in silence Sadie felt sure she could
hear the tiny sound of something precious breaking.

'You should have trusted me,' Leon told her angrily,
confirming her thoughts. 'But, no…'

Battling against her tears, Sadie gazed at him.

'Yes, you're right—I should,' she agreed quietly. 'But that goes both ways, Leon. We're two people who feel very strongly about certain things inside ourselves. I love you, and—'

'And I damn well love *you*,' Leon growled, giving her a look that made her ache to run into his arms and demand to be told that nothing else mattered other than that love.

But even love could not shut out reality and the world for ever. Buried problems had a way of growing and erupting, and if she and Leon could not reach a compromise... if they could not trust one another now, when their love was new...

'I asked Lebrun for his opinion because I wanted to come to you and tell you that I had changed my mind. I wanted to give you that change of mind as a gift of my love, Sadie.'

'I would rather you had given me your trust and treated me as an equal, not as a child to be given "gifts",' Sadie told him huskily.

But somehow she had moved, and so had he, and they were once more in each other's arms. From there it was just a few short, passionate moves to the bed, their discarded clothing littering the floor as they took refuge in the thing that bound them most securely together both physically and emotionally.

Through the blur of her tears Sadie saw the scratches she had left on Leon's back, scarlet weals of passion, inflicted in an agony of ecstasy he had induced and shared.

'We can't go on like this,' she whispered in despair. 'How can we be like this with one another when we don't trust each other? What's happening to us now is killing me, Leon, and I'm afraid that it will kill our love as well.'

'I know what you're saying,' Leon agreed. 'We need to start afresh, Sadie. Without any hidden agenda between us. I want you to create a new scent for Francine, but you will have to create it within a certain budget. You need time to think about whether or not you want to do that. And you need time to learn to trust me as well. What do you say to us having three months apart? I know how I feel about you, but you have to trust me, Sadie, and right now I don't believe that you do.'

'Three months apart sounds a good idea to me,' Sadie told him hollowly.

She was lying! Oh, how she was lying! The very thought of spending three *hours* apart from Leon right now was almost more than she could bear, but her pride would not allow her to say so. Why hadn't he just talked to her, instead of consulting Lebrun? Didn't *he* trust *her*?

Listening to Sadie agree to his plan, Leon clenched his jaw. How could he be such a fool? Right now what he longed to do more than anything else was pick Sadie up and carry her off somewhere he could have her all to himself—and for ever!

CHAPTER THIRTEEN

SADIE'S hand trembled as she stoppered the small precious bottle and wrapped it carefully in bubble wrap.

Her ticket was booked and there was no way she was going to give in to the nervousness and self-doubt that were making her hands tremble so much.

But what if, when she got to France, Leon reminded her that it was only three weeks since they had last been together and refused to see her? What if he insisted that they stick to their agreement not to see one another for three months? Or what if he had changed his mind altogether and simply no longer wanted her? What if...?

Sadie impatiently dismissed her wayward thoughts. Her flight was booked and her bag packed. Now all she needed to do was to place this precious phial of hope and love and compromise in her bag.

She was waiting in the departure lounge when her mobile rang. Answering it, she way surprised to hear Mary's voice.

'Sadie, where are you?' Mary demanded.

'At the airport,' Sadie replied. 'My flight has just been called, Mary.' She stood up to go and join the queue lining up for boarding.

'Stop right where you are,' she heard Mary urging. 'And if you aren't sitting down then I think you ought to be!' she added dramatically, pausing theatrically before continuing, 'You've got a visitor, Sadie.'

'A visitor?'

Sadie felt her hand start to tremble and then her whole

body as the small burst of aching disbelief inside her flowered warmly into hope.

Her mouth dry, she begged. 'Is it…is it Leon, Mary?'

It couldn't be, of course, and she was every kind of fool for even thinking that it might be, but…

'You'd just better come home,' Mary answered her obliquely. 'And you'd better get back here fast, because if you don't I might just be tempted to make off with him myself.'

It was the longest drive of Sadie's life! Mary hadn't said specifically that it was Leon who was her visitor, but Sadie hoped and prayed with every mile passing that it was. And that he would wait. And that he would listen. And that he would still want her. And… Her heart jerked, the uneven beat sending her pulse-rate scattering live bolts of nervous excitement through her body.

Please let it be Leon.

It was dark when she finally arrived home, and at first Sadie didn't see the dusty black Mercedes pulled to one side of her drive.

She was still focusing on it when the door of the house opened and Leon came walking out. How had he got in? Sadie momentarily wondered. Mary, of course! She had a spare key!

'Le—'

She didn't even get as far as finishing saying his name before she was dragged into his arms and kissed until she could hardly breathe.

'It *is* you. You *are* here!' she whispered shakily She was too thrilled to bother to hide her joy. 'Mary wouldn't say, but I hoped, and… Leon. Mmm…' She protested as he started to kiss her again, until somehow she discovered that they were both inside her house and the door was closed firmly behind them, shutting out the outside world.

'Let me look at you,' Leon demanded rawly, cupping her face and studying her features. 'You've lost weight,' he accused her gruffly.

'A little,' Sadie admitted, still breathless from his kisses. Inside her body the ache of longing which had begun pulsing there long before she had even got as far as the airport, never mind learned that Leon was here in her home, had become a demanding urge of embarrassing intensity. To try to ease it she shifted her weight from one foot to the other, and then gasped as she inadvertently bumped into him.

The feel of him against her sent the pulsing ache into hungry overdrive. Helplessly her hand went to his chest, then his waist before moving lower, unable to wait for the feel of the erection she could already see pushing against his jeans.

'Sadie,' she heard him growl protestingly, but she was beyond listening—had been beyond anything but satisfying her need for him from the moment she had seen him walking towards her.

She felt him tense and then shudder as she touched him, his reaction making her bolder—bold enough, in fact, to hold his gaze with her own as he groaned and covered her hand with his.

Now it was his gaze that was imprisoning her, just as it was her turn to shudder in mute response to the need they were both feeling.

'What you're doing right now, Sadie, is just about enough to push me over the edge,' Leon warned her huskily, bending his head to brush her lips with his own as he added, 'So if that isn't what you want...'

Purposefully he lifted his hand from hers, and just as

purposefully Sadie left hers where it was, covering the bulge under his jeans.

He had stopped kissing her and was simply looking at her with those dizzying green eyes. She started to tremble, and then flicked her tongue-tip nervously against her lips. As she did so for some reason her gaze dropped to Leon's crotch.

A raw sound like a cross between a roar and a groan warned her that she had tripped the danger switch, but before she could do anything Leon had grabbed hold of her, picking her up and swinging her into his arms.

'Which way is the bedroom?' he demanded thickly. 'And you'd better tell me damned quick, Sadie, otherwise it's going to have to be that kitchen table I can see right through there.'

As Sadie nodded numbly in the direction of the hallway leading to the stairs Leon acknowledged that he no longer gave a single damn about Francine or even Myrrh, and that right now the only thing…the only person that mattered to him was the woman he was holding in his arms. And he fully intended telling her so. There weren't going to be any more misunderstandings, no more misinformation! From now on he was planning to tell her every day of their lives how much he loved her.

How could he ever have risked losing her?

'You can't carry me all the way upstairs, Leon!' Sadie protested, but she still clung to him, revelling in the close contact she was enjoying.

'You just watch me!' he told her. 'On second thoughts, the kitchen table it is. There isn't any way I'm about to let you go! Not now, Sadie, and not ever.'

When he laid her down on her long pine table Sadie managed to find the conscience to remind him, 'About Francine, Leon…'

'Francine, nothing,' Leon growled. 'Right now the only perfume that's on my mind, Sadie, is yours!' he emphasised in a muffled voice, and he buried his face against her throat and started to kiss his way along it, unfastening the buttons on her shirt as he did so.

When she felt him slip his hand inside it and peel back the fabric of her bra to reveal the hard point of her nipple Sadie shuddered in wanton delight.

'You like this?' Leon demanded, watching her reaction as he rubbed his thumb against the aching crest of flesh. 'Like it?'

Sadie wondered hazily if Leon could translate the whimpered sound of pleasure she made, but patently he could, because he made a deep satisfied response in his own throat and then bent his lips to her breast, urging her thickly, 'And this? Do you like this too, Sadie?'

As Sadie's body arched, she frantically pulled open Leon's shirt. Her hands clung to his shoulders, her nails digging helplessly into his flesh, and Sadie could only give an incoherent moan. But Leon didn't need to hear any words. The way she was responding to him told him everything he needed to know.

The instant Leon's free hand stroked between her legs Sadie parted them. Inside her head she was already anticipating what was to come, her mind full of remembered images of intense sensuality.

Leon was tugging her jeans free of her legs, kneeling up on the table, his torso exposed where his shirt had been ripped open, Sadie recognised, her eyes widening as she stared at the torn fabric. Had she done that? And those scratches she could just see on his shoulder…had she inflicted those?

Leon had finished removing her jeans. He bent to remove her thin lace low-rise briefs.

Sadie closed her eyes in wanton pleasure as she felt the heat of his breath against her skin. Leon was sliding his hands beneath the lace. Her breath caught in her throat on a sob of pleasure.

'What is it, Sadie?' Leon was demanding huskily.

She could feel the heat of his breath on the soft triangle of curls beneath the lace. And then she could feel the light brush of his lips, teasing her, tantalising her with their promise of what she was already aching for...

'You want this?' he whispered, as his hands tugged away the lace and she was free to spread her legs in a wide vee of liquid female longing, inviting him to part the swollen lips of her sex and taste the sweet juice of her love.

The touch of Leon's tongue against the eager ridge of flesh that was her sensual centre sent Sadie wild. The firm lap of his tongue was taking her to heaven—beyond heaven, she acknowledged, as her body twisted and convulsed and the pleasure built up inside her to the point where she knew she was not going to be able to control it.

Leon's tongue lapped and stroked until Sadie could bear no more. Her whole body clenched, the muscles in her thighs tightening against Leon's hands as he held her.

As the first spasm of her orgasm began Leon raised his head and looked at her, watching her pleasure, making her focus wide-eyed on his gaze as it held her and demanded that she expose herself to him totally and completely.

As the quivers finally eased out of her body Sadie remembered there was something she had to tell him. Something important. Looking at him, she whispered with love-drugged urgency, 'Leon, the Myrrh formula—'

'Not now.' He stopped her, shaking his head and lowering his body to rest alongside her own. Tenderly he cupped her chin and started to kiss her, little gentle kisses that melted her insides.

'There's something I want to tell you first. I love you, and I need you, and if it means giving up the whole damn conglomerate to have you in my life then that is what I intend to do!'

'Oh, Leon!' Sadie protested mistily.

The look in his eyes as he bent over her and kissed her made her own prick with tears.

Slowly he released her mouth, his attention distracted by the sudden tightening of the nipple closest to him. Leon rewarded its demand with the lazy brush of his lips and the not so lazy lap of his tongue.

Immediately Sadie curled her toes, a small gasp of shocked pleasure parting her lips. Surely not again? Not so…so…immediately and intensely?

She made another small sound and reached for Leon.

The feel of him inside her filled her with a pleasure which went way beyond anything physical. Just holding him there was surely the most intense emotional experience she had ever had, Sadie acknowledged.

'More, Leon,' she demanded with female hunger. 'More…yes…just like that. Just like that…' she moaned as she urged him deeper and deeper within her, wrapping him tightly with the wet warmth of her flesh.

'Sadie!' Leon warned her, but her body was already eager for his climax, matching it and capturing him as he pulsed thickly inside her.

She was almost asleep when Leon pulled her up and they made their way up to bed. He tucked her into his side and pulled the bedclothes over them. But even in her sleep Sadie was not prepared to let him go.

Curled into his body, she rested one of her hand on

him. Not that she needed to hold him. Before he had fallen asleep Leon had thrown a possessive male leg over Sadie's body, imprisoning her where he intended to keep her. At his side. For ever.

When Sadie woke up she was on her own, the side of the bed next to her empty and cold—but nowhere near as cold as her heart.

Frantically she threw back the bedclothes and rushed to the window. The Mercedes was still outside!

Then she heard a sound from downstairs. Quickly she looked for something to put on. The first thing that caught her eye was Leon's discarded shirt. Pulling it on, she paused to breathe in the smell of him.

As she tried to fasten it up she realised that one of the buttons was missing and that one of the buttonholes was torn. Guiltily she remembered how that had happened! She had done it last night, in her eagerness to get to Leon's body!

Padding downstairs, she went into the kitchen, where she could smell coffee brewing. But Leon wasn't there. And then she saw him across the hallway in her sitting room. Holding her grandmother's photograph.

Even though she could have sworn she had not made a sound, he turned and looked at her.

'Your grandmother?' he asked.

Silently Sadie nodded her head.

Putting the photograph back, Leon came towards her.

'Where were you going yesterday?' he asked.

Sadie looked at him

'To find you,' she admitted. And, turning away from him, she went to where she had left her bag the previous evening. Opening it, she removed the bubble-wrapped packet. 'And to give you this,' she added, handing the package to him.

'What is it?' Frowning, Leon unwrapped it and stared at the small glass phial in his hand.

'I...' Sadie took a deep breath. 'You weren't the only one looking for...for a compromise. It's a new Myrrh perfume,' she told him huskily. 'I...I made it here in my workshop. It's a...' She stopped and discovered that her whole body was shaking. Lifting her head, she looked at him. 'It's a blend of raw material and...and synthetics.' She bit her lip.

For a long time she thought he simply wasn't going to speak. His whole attention was concentrated on the small bottle he was holding. But then suddenly he raised his head, and in the green eyes and on the black lashes Sadie could see quite openly the glitter of strong male tears.

'You did this for me?' Leon demanded.

'For us,' Sadie corrected him, her own gaze blurring.

'Oh, Sadie.' Leon groaned, kissing her softly and then saying against her lips, 'Sadie, I love you. Will you marry me? You'd better,' he advised when she looked at him.

'For one thing I just couldn't bear it if you don't, and for another...' He bent his head and whispered in her ear, 'After last night, I feel in nine months' time there could be a very good reason why you and I should be man and wife!'

'A baby?' Sadie blinked away her tears.

'Mmm...we could try for twins if you like,' Leon teased her.

It took several seconds for his meaning to sink through Sadie's euphoric happiness. When it did she gave him an old-fashioned look.

'Certainly not,' she told him primly. 'Well, at least not until I've had a cup of coffee…'

'You can have a cup of coffee…when I've had you…' Leon promised sexily.

EPILOGUE

'AND so what have you called the new baby?' the excited reporter asked Sadie eagerly.

Bright-eyed, she looked at Leon, who was standing by her side.

'Well, I think we've decided on Petit Bébé.' Sadie answered her, straight-faced.

She and Leon had worked hard to come up with an original name for the range of baby products they were launching under the Francine name. The range had gone into production just about the same time as Sadie herself, and the results of both efforts were on display in the Grasse house now. The Petit Bébé range of babycare products in their attractive modern packaging, and the equally modern and attractively packaged identical twin daughters Sadie had given birth to six weeks before.

'See, I told you it could be twins,' Leon had murmured when Sadie had gone for the scan which had revealed the fact that she was carrying two babies.

And despite the fact that she was a recently married woman and a mother-to-be Sadie had blushed deeply at the look in his eyes, remembering just how and where those babies had been conceived.

'I wonder which of them is the kitchen table baby,' Leon whispered teasingly to her when the press conference was over.

'Neither or both,' Sadie responded firmly. 'After all, they are identical twins.'

Still smiling at her, Leon bent his head to kiss her.

The world's bestselling romance series.

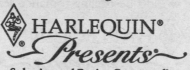

HARLEQUIN® Presents~

Seduction and Passion Guaranteed!

MILLIONAIRE MARRIAGES

When the million-dollar question is "Will you marry me?"

Coming Soon in Harlequin Presents...
An exciting duet by talented author

Sandra Field

Don't miss...

May 2004: The Millionaire's Marriage Demand #2395
Julie Renshaw is shocked when Travis Strathern makes an outrageous demand: marriage! She is overwhelmingly attracted to him—but is she ready to marry him for convenience? Travis is used to getting his own way—but Julie makes certain he won't this time...unless their marriage is based on love as well as passion....

June 2004: The Tycoon's Virgin Bride #2401
One night Jenessa's secret infatuation with tycoon Bryce Laribee turned to passion—but the moment he discovered she was a virgin he walked out! Twelve years later, the attraction between them is just as mind-blowing, and Bryce is determined to finish what they started. But Jenessa has a secret or two....

Available wherever Harlequin books are sold.

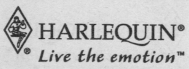

HARLEQUIN®
Live the emotion™

Visit us at www.eHarlequin.com

HPMILMAR

The world's bestselling romance series.

HARLEQUIN®
Presents

Seduction and Passion Guaranteed!

OUTBACK KNIGHTS
Marriage is their mission!

From bad boys—to powerful,
passionate protectors!

Three tycoons from the Outback
rescue their brides-to-be....

Coming soon in Harlequin Presents:
Emma Darcy's exciting new trilogy

Meet Ric, Mitch and Johnny—once three Outback bad
boys, now rich and powerful men. But these sexy city
tycoons must return to the Outback to face a new
challenge: claiming their women as their brides!

MAY 2004: THE OUTBACK MARRIAGE RANSOM #2391
JULY 2004: THE OUTBACK WEDDING TAKEOVER #2403
NOVEMBER 2004: THE OUTBACK BRIDAL RESCUE #2427

*"Emma Darcy delivers a spicy love story...
a fiery conflict and a hot sensuality."*
—Romantic Times

Available wherever Harlequin books are sold.

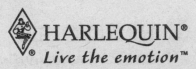

HARLEQUIN®
Live the emotion™

Visit us at www.eHarlequin.com

Coming Next Month

HARLEQUIN Presents

THE BEST HAS JUST GOTTEN BETTER!

#2391 THE OUTBACK MARRIAGE RANSOM Emma Darcy
At sixteen, Ric Donato wanted Lara Seymour—but they were worlds apart. Years later he's a city tycoon, and now he can have anything he wants.... Lara is living a glamorous life with another man, but Ric is determined to have her—and he'll do whatever it takes....

#2392 THE STEPHANIDES PREGNANCY Lynne Graham
Cristos Stephanides wanted Betsy Mitchell the moment he saw her, shy and prim in her chauffeur's outfit, at the wheel of his limousine.... However, the Greek tycoon hadn't bargained on being kidnapped—along with Betsy—and held captive on an Aegean island!

#2393 A SICILIAN HUSBAND Kate Walker
When Terrie Hayden met Gio Cardella she knew that there was something between them. Something that was worth risking everything for. But the proud Sicilian didn't want to take that risk. He had no idea what force kept dragging him back to her door....

#2394 THE DESERVING MISTRESS Carole Mortimer
May Calendar has spent her life looking after her sisters and running the family business—and she's determined not to let anyone take it away from her! Especially not arrogant tycoon Jude Marshall! But sexy, charming Jude is out to wine and dine her—how can she resist...?

#2395 THE MILLIONAIRE'S MARRIAGE DEMAND Sandra Field
Julie Renshaw is shocked when Travis Strathern makes an outrageous demand: marriage! She is very attracted to him—but is she ready to marry for convenience? Travis always gets his own way—but Julie makes it clear that their marriage must be based on love as well as passion....

#2396 THE DESERT PRINCE'S MISTRESS Sharon Kendrick
Multimillionaire Darian Wildman made an instant decision about beautiful Lara Black—he had to have her! Their mutual attraction was scorching! Then Darian made a discovery that would change both their lives. He was the illegitimate heir to a desert kingdom—and a prince!